Shattered Dreams

ALLAN HUDSON

Enjoy
Allan.

South Branch Scribbler
410-3400 Principale Ouest
Dieppe, NB
Canada
E1A 9E7

sbscribbler@gmail.com
www.southbranchscribbler.com

eBook ISBN – 978-1-988291-19-2
Paperback ISBN – 978-1-988291-18-5

SHATTERED FIGURINE

"Fantastic read. Allan is a great wordsmith to say the least. For such a small book, it packs a heck of a wallop." - PIERRE ARSENEAULT – AUTHOR OF POPLAR FALLS: THE DEATH OF CHARLIE BAKER

SHATTERED LIVES

"WOW! This book is packed with action from start to finish. Jo Naylor's vacation/relocation turns out to be a cause she never expected to become embroiled in. Enough said, check it out." – AUTHOR CHERYL SHENCK

FATHER

"A quick read that carries a punch. There are no wasted words in this tale about family and the effects of war on relationships. The characters are real and relatable." - DARLENE FOSTER. AUTHOR OF THE AMANDA SERIES.

THE ALEXANDERS 1911 -1920 VOL. 1

"Mr. Hudson weaves a wonderful tale of love and endurance and it is easy to become entwined with Dominic and those he meets along the way. I look forward in anticipation to the next chapter in the life of the Alexanders." - SHARON BEDDOES

To Gloria. My one true love.

CONTENTS

ACKNOWLEDGMENTS

Thank you, always to Gloria, for allowing me the space and time to pursue my hobby.

Thank you to my family for their ongoing support.

Adam, Chris & Mireille, Mark, Matthieu, Natasha & Damien.

Thank you to my dearest friends, Gracia & Allen Williston for always being there.

Thank you to Sandra Bunting for editing.

Thank you to Donna Dean Photography for the great cover.

Thank you to Jeremy McLean for formatting.

Thank you to the following individuals for their ongoing support:

John Roberts – Chapters Moncton. Emily Ann Mercer of Dog Eared Books. James Fisher of The Miramichi Reader. Author MJ LaBeff. Author Sally Cronin. Author Janice Spina. Author Marjorie Mallon. Bernie & Jacinthe Blanchard. Gail Brown. Linda Vautour. Carol & Christine Beers. June Hebert. Stephen Shortall. Theresa LeBlanc. Susan Jardine.

CHAPTER 1

JANUARY 11, ORLY AIRPORT, PARIS

Arriving from the tropical weather in Thailand, Jo Naylor doesn't care for the icy rain falling outside. She's not going to let it bother her though, except she's not dressed for the cooler weather. When the plane approaches the airport, and the Eiffel Tower, the iconic landmark that lured her to Paris comes into view, the excitement of the metropolis grips her. She feels giddy thinking of seeing the famed city. It makes her think of birthday parties when she was little and the anticipation feels the same.

When she passes through customs, she tries to remain aloof even though her nerves are on edge, her palms sweaty. Authorities have an interest in Jo Naylor back in Canada. This is the first time she's used this particular passport so she keeps repeating the name to herself to memorize it - Jane Taylor, Jane Taylor. The passport looks used, a perfect forgery. Thankfully, this morning, there is a lineup twenty deep at each customs wicket, and the agents seem to be rushing people through. The older agent barely glances at it, pecks at her keyboard. When no flags show up, he stamps an empty page, waving Jo through with a head motion, already concentrating on the next in line.

Yesterday morning, in Kiri Kahn, Jo said goodbye to her former partner from Canada where they worked the streets as detectives. She and Adam Thorne had put a lot of bad people behind bars. Hoping to bring her home from Thailand to clear her name, he ended up helping her and a PI save some children when he found her. He was the last

1

person she had expected to see there. Thorne always brought out Naylor's good side. Their personalities fit. She remembers his remark when they parted at the airport.

"Try and stay out of trouble this time, Jo. I'm not always going to be around to cover your back. But when I get home, I'll tell them I couldn't find you."

She had loved her job, that is until they had to arrest her father, the prime suspect in a killing spree that she and Thorne had been investigating. The horror of what she discovered still clutches her heart and makes her angry. Questioning her own response to his madness, she sometimes regrets what she did before she fled the country, giving it all up.

She can't go back. Not yet. Not until she can reconcile with the past. It's inconvenient to travel under a false name and yet she loves the drama, like being in one of the the spy novels she reads. For the right money, with forged documents, you get a new life, in both the real world and the web world, at least in all the places nosy people might look. She's ready for whatever the future brings.

Right now she has to buy a winter jacket before she leaves the airport. She's wearing jeans, a T-shirt and a blouse under a zippered fleece and a pair of running shoes, all in a similar shade of black and grey. She didn't take a winter coat or boots to Thailand; she doesn't invite vegan friends to a barbecue either. Climbing the stairs back to the departure level, she searches for a clothing store. She knows whatever she finds will cost a lot more than what a department store in the city would charge for the same garment. People like her are their livelihood.

Thank goodness most of the store staff speak English, as her high school French is shaky. Forty-five minutes later she's wearing a ski jacket by some designer she's not familiar with. It reminds her of her Mountain Coop jacket she had at one time, charcoal with black accents and lots of pockets. To complete the outfit, she tucks her hair under a black baseball hat bearing the French Football Federation logo and pulls on over-the-ankle leather boots laced up in front. She's good. Tugging along her suitcase and a backpack, she looks for the exit.

As she waits for her bus at the periphery of the exit doors under an overhang, she watches and listens to all the people around her. The noise level is high, with a cacophony of voices in multiple languages, people yelling for attention, happy greetings, long goodbyes and babies crying. So many people. The odour of sweet colognes, wet clothes and vehicle exhaust wanders with the crowd. People are in a hurry. She's glad to be here but looking forward to the quiet of the bed and breakfast she has reserved close to the airport, five or six kilometers away. She can take a bus to a terminal in Creteil and someone is picking her up there. The inn is on the rim of the village, an older building, formerly a convent.

It's shortly after lunch hour when she arrives at the inn. The gentleman who picked her up was a slight man with a bent back and a warm smile. He had to keep pushing his glasses back up his thin nose. The inn is a square set of buildings with cloisters on the inside facing a garth. The stone architecture is a century old design of brick and slate. It looks like the grandfather of nearby structures. Checking in takes a few minutes, and soon she's unpacking in what was formerly a nun's cell. It's decorated with frilly lace and sunshine, pictures of mountains and streams. Paying a week in advance, she wants to plan the rest of her time but right now she's starving. The owner showed her where the dining room is. A buffet of cold cuts, cheeses and bread, along with salads is offered. Taking her note pad, she hurries off to eat.

Sitting at the table with her lunch, a plate of prosciutto, brie, parmesan, genoa salami and fresh baked bread. Her stomach growls at the feast. There are three other people in the dining room even though it's later than the usual lunch hour. After making a sandwich of meats and cheese, she pulls her notebook closer and grabs her pen.

She jots down things she wants to do. Today she just wants to rest, get over the jet lag.

1. Bus to Paris – walk the streets.
2. Find room for budget of 250 euros a month. If not possible, stay here?
3. A painting class?
4. Buy long johns (or is it long janes???)
5. Find bank to deal with and make withdrawal.

When she takes the last bite of her second sandwich, she finishes her coffee and nods at her list.

"Enough for today."

"*Pardonnez-moi?*"

Startled by the voice behind her, she turns to see a man sitting at the table behind her. She can't stop looking at his cobalt eyes, guarded,

3

with a glint of curiosity on the edges and shadowed by lifelines at the temples. Caught talking to herself Jo reddens and tries her high school French.

"*J'ai regret Monsieur, je ne parle pas beaucoup français.*"

"*Ah, oui, une Anglaise.* Excuse me, Miss, but you commented a moment ago and I was wondering if you were speaking to me."

A softening of his eyes accompanies a wide smile.

"At least, I was hoping such a pretty lady was talking to me."

Jo's cheeks continue to blossom. She's used to compliments as she's an attractive woman but this man is definitely flirting with her. And he's old enough to be her father.

"I was actually talking to myself but thank you."

"*Oui*, it is good to have an audience that listens to our comments with interest."

He's quite cheerful and the hardness she noticed before disappears with his light laughter. A row of straight white teeth and smooth cheeks make him appear younger, but with the thinning grey hair, she guesses he's close to seventy.

"Yes, I suppose it is."

She likes the man. Something about his demeanor attracts her. She stretches backward to offer her hand.

"Name's Jane, Jane Taylor. And you are?"

"Maxime, but my English friends call me Max."

She raises her brows at his hint of familiarity.

"Are we friends?"

"I think we can be. Are you Canadian? I noticed the maple leaf on your lapel pin."

Jo is leery of divesting too much personal information to strangers. He seems harmless enough. Still, she lies to him.

"Yes, from Winnipeg. On holidays."

He pushes his empty plate aside and stands with his mug in his hand.

"May I join you?"

She isn't able to stifle a yawn.

"Excuse me. I must warn you, Max, I arrived here on a red eye from Thailand and I'm beat. Not sure if I'll be good company. But please sit and we can finish our coffee together."

Max sweeps around the table to sit across from her. She thinks him jaunty with his cheerful expression, the form fitting white shirt and hounds-tooth sport coat, a black silk scarf knotted at his neck. The only thing missing is a beret.

"So, Jane Taylor, what will you do on your first day in our lovely city?"

She turns her notepad so he can read it. Leaning ahead, he smiles when he reaches number four.

"I can help you with number five. If you are walking, turn left off the driveway and five minutes later you will be at a stop sign, turn right. It is the second building. Number two on your list, you won't find a room in the city for two-fifty. You could stay here for two hundred euros a month. It is their off season and they welcome longer stays. I know the owner well. You must bargain with him. He loves it. The buses are cheap. The metro is close. The food is delicious."

He waves his hands as if to say what more could you want. She yawns again.

"Ah Jane, I can see you are tired. Let me be quick. I don't know the expression *long janes* but I think you mean *calecons*, so, when you leave the bank, turn right a few stores further and there is a lingerie shop. As for paint classes, my dear friend Aurora is an artist, she will know these things. And lastly, may I offer myself as your guide after you are settled in? Tomorrow I am off to Amsterdam for two days until Monday, but nothing would please me more than to introduce you to our beautiful city."

Jo sits up a little straighter, caught off guard and uncertain by the offer. She looks at him directly. She's good at reading people from her work as a cop and doesn't see any deceit or mischief in him. But she's only known him for twenty minutes. Her reverie is abruptly broken and she's startled out of her indecision by a honeyed female voice.

"If you're wondering if you can trust him, I can assure you, Monsieur Maxime Brisbois is a perfect gentleman. Plus, he knows the heart of the city. Pardon my intrusion."

Jo turns to the voice to see a woman in her early thirties, close to her age, clad in jeans, a black T-shirt and an apron with the inn's logo on it. She is clearing Max's table. She winks at Jo and carries on. He voices what his hands implied earlier.

"What more could you ask for?"

Jo laughs at his silly grin.

"Ok then, Max. You're on. I'll do these errands first thing in the morning and get settled. Shall we meet here for breakfast Tuesday morning, say around nine?"

"*Non, non*, my dear. If we are off to the city, let us get a full day. If you are an early riser, meet me in the foyer at seven. I know a quaint spot where we can dine on fresh croissants, fruit and unbelievable quiche. Make your arrangements and purchase what you need but there are many fashionable shops where you will have much more fun. I'll point out the attractions you can see on your own. For the Louvre you need more than a day. And better yet, we may run into my artist friend, Aurora. *Bon!* It is done. I must leave you to your rest. Here, Tuesday morning at seven."

With that, he leaves Jo dizzy with his last comments; he was speaking so fast. Gathering her shoulder bag and notepad she proceeds to the stairway, her eyelids heavy, and thoughts in her head swirling of how nice her bed is going to feel. Remembering the glee on his face when she said she would join him; she expects her day with Max will be anything but boring.

CHAPTER 2

Jo is nursing a coffee when Max joins her at 6:48 AM. They are leaving in a few minutes. Max forgot his hat and returns to his room to retrieve it. Jo's waiting for him at the reception area of the inn. Two heavy oak doors with large windows offer egress and Jo studies her reflection in the glass. She likes the new jacket and the white toque she has pulled down to her eyebrows. A few stray hairs escape from the bottom in the back, which she tries to straighten out. Sometimes she misses the ponytail she left in Thailand but likes the ease of her hair being shorter. Thinking her hips too wide, she chides herself for loving cheese so much. Her black jeans have a soft patina along the edges from many washings and she loves them the most. A beige cashmere sweater is buttoned over a white, sleeveless silk blouse.

Hearing footsteps behind her, she turns to see Max with a black beret at a forty-five-degree angle. She remembers their first encounter and thinking a beret would fit his persona. As handsome as he looks, she can't stop from laughing. Max stops mid-stride a few feet from her and looks around to see what must be so funny. She doesn't want to insult him so has to think fast. A black and white cat comes to her rescue, sitting up on the welcome desk, pawing a writing pen that spins when she bats it.

"The cat knows how to entertain itself."

"*Ah oui*, Miss *Gâté*, which means spoiled. She has the run of the inn and grounds. Quite friendly. Shall we be off?"

The weather report is calling for a high of ten degrees Celsius and uninterrupted sunshine but later tonight for clouds to settle in from the west, possible rain. They set out into the early light and are greeted with extended shadows, the new day shining over their shoulders like a friend. The bus to the metro is only five minutes. Paris' subway and elevated train system, the Metro, is extremely efficient. During the high-speed transit, Jo learns that Max is an author of non-fiction. Formerly a civil defense lawyer, he now makes his living writing about and critiquing law judgements and settlements in different countries. Outspoken for his opinions of current cases and likely outcomes, he is often proven right. It is not your usual best seller material but useful enough that thousands of law offices make his writings part of their libraries.

He lost his wife to cancer four years ago, sold his home and travels as often as he can. His only child is a professor at the University of Stuttgart in Germany where he teaches political science. He is married to another professor and they have no children. Max keeps a permanent room at the inn.

When he politely asks of Jo's past, she sidesteps the issue and feeds him the barest of information other than she was a police officer. He doesn't need to know she's a walking death threat, able to bring the biggest man down with her bare hands, and that from fifty feet she can hit a bullseye with a pistol nine times out of ten. She answers his queries informing him she was a beat cop in a small city, with not too much action, and now using her inheritance to see the world.

They get off the Metro near Champ des Mars and he takes her to a small diner, owned by a retired couple. Specializing in breakfast only, they close at eleven. Tucked in between two ancient buildings of brick and stucco, the *Café Mercier* is a busy spot with mostly older couples dining and gossiping. He orders for them both, lattes, Quiche Lorraine and fruit filled crepes. During breakfast he relays his feelings about Paris, his love for the city evident in every word and expression, always relayed with the brightest of smiles. With hand gestures and enthusiasm, he talks about the arts, the museums, the Eiffel Tower, the famed Champs-Élysées, the music and most fervently in his descriptions – the people.

After dining they walk to the Eiffel Tower. Referring it to it as *La dame de fer* (The Iron Lady) which local people call it, he explains the history, the erecting of the monument, its glory. He often refers to the builder, Gustave Eiffel and shares a rumour that Eiffel also designed a house of iron in Iquitos, Peru, which is the largest city in the world not accessible by road. They find they both share an interest in the Incas and their gold. They spend a couple of hours there and brave the cold to climb to a high platform from where he points out the arrondissements and sites she needs to see to better understand the city and the people's *joie de vivre*. He passes her a small map of attractions and has outlined his favourites that she should visit, Le Jardin des Palais Royal, Place de la Concorde, Musée de l'Orangerie, Musée Rodin and the Grand Palais to name a few, and of course, the Louvre.

After spending the morning at the Eiffel Tower, strolling along the Champs-Élysées and visiting the Arc des Triomphe, they visit the 4th arrondissement. Max takes her to a small café, *La Petite Cuisine*, secluded amongst boutiques, gay bars, art galleries and the most colourful people of Paris - the artists, writers, poets, sculptors and fashion designers. The cobbled streets are lined with pleasant coloured buildings standing shoulder to shoulder. The storied side-streets are exactly what she'd pictured Paris to be. Jo comments on the amazing architecture and age of the buildings. Max tells her their age is often mentioned in centuries, many older than Canada as a country. Max introduces her to Madame Trembley, the owner, who is famous for her *terrine* and pastries. They dine on the meat delicacy with fresh baguette, and cold soup, and the smoothest white wine she's ever tasted. They spend an hour and a half eating slowly, with Max laughing and joking with the staff and other regulars, having a wonderful time introducing his new friend from Canada. They complete their meal with éclairs and strong coffee laced with cognac.

By mid-afternoon, feeling a bit tipsy, they venture through the narrow streets blustering with decorative awnings and Jo makes her purchases. She buys two touristy type T-shirts and finds a new book by Canadian phenomenon, Beth Powning, laughing all the while at Max's many jokes and pondering his intellectual forays into art and writing, his favourite subjects. He insists that she learn French so she can read Hugo's masterpiece, *Les Misérables* in its original text. By five-thirty, it's almost dark, her feet hurt. She's exhausted and laden down with shopping bags. Max, more animated than ever, shows no sign of tiring. When they stop at a water fountain, Jo tries not to complain but she'd like to go home.

"I think I've had enough for today, Max. I don't think I can walk a step more. I'm beat. You're a hard man to keep up with. Where do you get your energy?"

"Je ne sais pas d'où ça vient. We must embrace each day, each moment, with élan. I'm having so much fun. You are such a charming lady, and a joy to be with. There are so many things I want to share with you. I know you are tired, Jane, but the best part of your day is yet to come."

Jo plops down on a wooden bench. Placing her parcels at her feet, she pats the seat next to her.

"Oh, Max, I've had such a pleasant day with you. It's not every visitor to your beautiful city that has a personal and knowledgeable guide. I am indebted to you but I need to rest. Sit with me for a minute. And what do you mean the best part?"

Max joins her and pats her on the knee. Adjusts his beret and tightens his collar. When he talks, his breath frosts around his words like they're special.

"A night life like no other. An evening of gaiety, enchanting music, a plethora of wines to choose from and stimulating intellect. But first let us be off to visit my artist friend I spoke of, Aurora. You can rest there and after we, all three, shall go to *La Grotte du Heros.*"

Giving into his eagerness, she follows him the three blocks to a stately three level stone building nestled between two similar edifices. The only differences are the colours, the boutiques on the main level and entryways. Aurora Deschamps has her studio, kitchen and living room on the second level, bedrooms and storage on the third. She responds to the intercom when Max pushes the buzzer. A soft voice answers. In English, Max reminds her of their rendezvous and says he has a guest. Aurora guesses first his guest is a female and secondly, an Anglaise.

"*Ah,* Mon chèr, *entrez, come in.*"

The stairway is narrow but brightly coloured with sconces of stained glass lighting the way. The door is already open when they reach her apartment and Aurora Deschamps is not what Jo expected. She's almost as tall as Jo, and willowy. Pushed behind her ears, her hair is long and curly, flowing to her shoulders. Beads of exotic wood, odd, polished stones and a gold cross hang from her neck. The multi-coloured dress flows almost to the floor. Jo thinks of Janis Joplin, but older. She's not pretty but the high cheekbones and dark eyes give her a worldly appeal. Her smile is welcoming.

In the entryway, Max introduces the ladies and Jo breathes in a peculiar scent of jasmine and marijuana. Aurora hugs Jo when introduced.

"Welcome to my humble *maison*, Jane. You're out and about with this old rascal and not in trouble yet? Perhaps it is too early."

Jo is charmed by Aurora's accent and Max laughs at the expected gibe.

"Oh, you're a fine one to talk. It seems to me that they are always your ideas that cause us the most trouble…ahem… like the wine glasses of our last rendezvous?"

"*Oui, oui,* but so much fun."

"The fun, as you call it, cost me over thirty euros for the broken glassware."

A scowl covers his face, but the ladies can tell he's only joking and Jo gets caught up in their cheerfulness. She hopes to hear more of the story.

"Let's not talk about our silly pranks in front of our guest, Max. She may get the wrong impression. But we do like to have fun, Jane. Life is too short to stay still. *Oui?*"

"Yes, I agree. Max has kept me on my feet all day. It's been marvelous fun but I need to sit for a while. You're so kind to invite us in, Aurora. And you have such a pretty name."

"*Merci*, Jane. I'm named for the Roman goddess of the dawn. But I fear I'm totally the opposite. Give me the nights, the crowded cafés, the city's dark and vacant streets to roam, the neighbourhoods that never sleep. Anyway, come into my living room for a sip of wine first. Perhaps something stronger. It's only a little after six. I have some *hors d'oeuvres et petite sandwich.* And then you can rest. Come."

They veer off the hallway to the left where a large living room is spread out around a fireplace on the outer wall facing the street. A tall narrow window is on each side, with the rest of the wall divided up into shelves holding books, trinkets, a small lamp and small oil paintings propped up on tiny easels. Above the fireplace is a large, framed canvas. Jo recognizes the style as knife painting. A woman is poised at the edge of a lake, undressing. The reflections and shimmers of the water beckon to her. An exquisite piece.

"How beautiful. This is your work, Aurora?"

"Yes, thank you, Jane. It's one of my favourites. I've been offered thousands of euros for it but the time to part with it has not yet arrived. Please, have a seat."

A couch and two chairs face the fireplace where a small log crackles, the flames dancing along the edges. A rectangular table of glass and wicker holds a bottle of wine and a tray with three glasses, a half full baggy of marijuana, an ashtray in the shape of a frog with an open mouth, a small wooden pipe laying on its side and an open book of matches. Aurora takes one of the chairs, Max the one opposite and Jo sits between them on the couch. Aurora pours wine. She fills the pipe, tamps it down, lights it up and draws on it to make sure it's lit. The she passes it to Max who has a hit and hands it questionably to Jo.

Being a cop was supposed to make her opposed to marijuana, but she knew several colleagues who used it at home or with close friends. She doesn't think possession should be illegal. She's tried it a few times and can take it or leave it but decides the excitement of the day calls for it. She takes small puffs because she's doesn't normally smoke. She coughs on the first one much to her companions' glee. The next ones are smoother, and she can taste a fruity hint of blueberry.

"Now Jane, tell me your story and how you ended up with this Lothario."

Max grins at the title and winks at Aurora. Jane sees admiration between the two, perhaps something more. She tells her story as best as she can with lies, lies she's rehearsed many times and will need to remember. Still, she offers as little information as she can. As the marijuana takes effect, she settles into the glow and laughs between sentences. Her mouth is dry from the smoke and she sips on her wine often. Forty-five minutes later, Jo is curled up on the couch, as dead to the world as a doorstop.

She wakes an hour later to the sounds of bedsprings singing and the moans of someone in the throes of passion. Confused at first, she catches on and remains frozen in her position, giggling into the cushion she lies upon. The old bugger, she thinks. She decides it's best to lie still and pretend she's sleeping until she hears footsteps in the apartment. Twenty minutes go by before Aurora is in the kitchen and from it sounds like her pouring another glass of wine. Jo tries sitting up, elbows on her knees and has to hold her head for a minute. She's feeling a little woozy, probably from the pot. The sleep is just what she needed.

She's disturbed by a tap on the shoulder. Aurora places a cup of steaming coffee and a small plate of pastries on the low table in front of the couch. She's changed her attire to a black knee length muslin skirt with uneven layers and a lacy hem. A low-necked light grey sweater leaves her shoulders bare, obvious she isn't wearing a bra. Her hair is tied back and pale pink lipstick adorns her sensuous lips. Very sexy.

"Here, *chère*, have some of this before we go out. Mustn't drink on an empty stomach.

"Thank you, Aurora. I need this but first I must use your washroom."

"I think Max is still in there but he won't be long. There's another upstairs if you like. First door on the left at the top."

"Ok, I'll use that one if you don't mind."

"Go, young lady. I'll nurse my wine for now."

When Jo returns, Max is sitting on the couch and the wine has been exchanged for a tall glass of dark liquid over ice cubes.

"Can I spike your coffee, Jane? A little Armagnac to sharpen the edge?"

"Sure, why not?"

He pours a healthy dollop from the fancy bottle while Aurora crumbles light brown hash into her pipe. Lighting it, she passes it to Jo.

"Only a couple of small tokes from this Jane. It's potent and we want you to last the night. It's almost nine and we can go in a little while."

The trio finish their respective drinks and pass the pipe. When nine-thirty rolls around, Aurora dons a black and white shawl and leads them out the door.

"Now, let's go and meet the night."

CHAPTER 3

Following the route back to where they were shopping earlier, amongst bars and cafes, Aurora leads them to *La Grotte des Heros*. On their way, if the cobbled streets and narrow ways are not enough to remind her of where she is, she gets a glimpse of the lit-up tip of the Eiffel Tower on the horizon when they pass near a park. The nightclub is nestled tightly between similar buildings, squeezed in shoulder to shoulder with other bars. Max informs her that the tall, narrow structure of quarried stone is two hundred years old. An awning in red hovers over the wide windows that are translucent, only offering shadows of the patrons as they move around. The entryway is recessed and lighted behind a heavy wooden door, circular on top. It reminds Jo of the door to Bilbo Baggins home in the shire. She titters at her thought of hobbits dancing inside.

When they enter, the premises are busy, while not full, for a Tuesday night. But then she realizes, this is Paris, a city of millions, why wouldn't it be? In the back, upon a narrow stage a black woman dressed in white jeans and a tight red T-shirt with a matching band in her ebony hair is singing a love ballad, one Jo recognizes from a Nat King Cole album she owned. The lady has a husky voice like Cassandra Wilson and is backed up by a tall black man playing a doghouse bass and a blonde man on the acoustic electric guitar. She's swaying, eyes closed, to her music as she sings. Jo is enthralled by the songstress and at how obvious it is that she loves what she's doing. Under the rhythm, voices and laughter combine in a low murmur.

The full-length bar of polished chrome and dark wood is long and rectangular. Tables line the right-hand wall that displays large black and white portraits of France's famous personalities or heroes. Victor Hugo, Charles De Gaulle, and Marquis de Lafayette are the only ones Jo recognizes. In front, there are matching swivel seats, most of them full. A hallway after the bar leads to washrooms and a red *Sortie/Exit* light sits above another door. Except for a postage size dance floor in front of the stage, the rest of the open area has waist high tables bolted to the floor where patrons stand and mingle. Lighting is low except over the stage where different lights rotate in pastel colours. A yeasty aroma of draft beer and the zest of champagne fills the air.

Max and Aurora seem to know everyone. Greeting individuals on their way toward the back, they introduce Jo to a dozen people. She only has a chance to say "*Bonsoir*" before they move her along. She'll never remember all their names. The euphoric feeling she's experiencing heightens her senses. She's tuned into the melody of the music and the liveliness of the crowd. Out of habit and encouraged by her buzz, she tries to check off something distinct about each person she meets: the old man with a chrysanthemum in his coat breast pocket, the girl with the freckles, the geeky guy with the frayed hair, the woman with the lined face. She meets all these characters before they even get settled. At their table another woman awaits them with open arms, hugs them all, even Jo who's not yet been introduced. Max does the honours.

"Brandy, this is Jane, Jane Taylor. Jane, this is Brandy Williams, a journalist of some note. And one of our dear friends."

She only comes up to Jo's shoulder. With her extra weight and tight shirt, Jo's envious of her curves. Her round face is unblemished and split with a happy smile. A slim nose holds a pair of tortoiseshell glasses making her bright eyes bigger. Jo likes her right away. When she speaks, Jo detects an Australian accent.

"Happy to meet you, Jane.

"Same here, Brandy.

They're interrupted by a young man, oozing with charm, who carries a tray and a damp cloth. He graces the ladies with the sweetest of compliments and offers Max a man-to-man wink while polishing their table. He takes their order and promises to be back before closing. Not knowing a word of what he said, Jo laughs along with the others, infected with the good cheer. Aurora reaches over to cover Jo's hand.

"Our waiter said it became much brighter in here since you arrived."

15

Not usually one to be taken in by a flirtatious comment, Jo, feeling foolish and hopes her blush can't be seen in the low light. Still, she likes the shine in the waiter's eyes and the gorgeous lashes she'd kill for.

"I think he's after a bigger tip."

"You catch on quick. Smart lady. But he is quite handsome and he knows it. And he's extremely friendly."

Brandy has taken the inside seat with Jo. While Jo is watching the stage where the lady and the bass player are singing Ella and Louis' "*Can't we be Friends*", Brandy addresses her as Jane. She doesn't get a response. Only a hand on the shoulder gets her attention.

"You were concentrating on the song so much, you didn't hear me, Jane."

Jo would kick herself if she could. She heard it and it didn't ring. She needs to remember Jane. Jane. Jane.

"Yes, sorry. I love this song. It's been a while since I've heard it and they do it so well. The bass player even has that husky voice of Louis'. What were you saying?"

Mr. Suave, the waiter, dashes over and sets them up with a frosted pitcher of sangria and four wine glasses. He flirts with Brandy while he pours their first drinks. Max gives him a credit card and makes a circle around the drinks.

"Hang on to that, Maurice, we'll likely be needing more."

Jo offers a toast.

"To my new friends. Thank you for making me feel so welcome. *Merci*."

Jo loves sangria. Diluted wine with a kiss of fruit, a good combo and welcome for her dry mouth.

"Mmmm. That's delicious. Thank you, Max."

"*Oui, merci*, Max."

"Cheers, Max."

Max turns in his seat to talk to the people behind him. Aurora is looking up at a lady stopped in the aisle who is chatting excitedly about something. Brandy turns to Jo.

"So, what are you doing in Paris, Jane?"

"My grandparents saved up money all their lives so they could travel. He passed away a year before his retirement and she lost both of her lower legs from cancer a year later. It didn't matter how much they saved, there would be no travelling. She gave me the money they saved on the condition I would travel as far as it can take me and to leave before she passed away. I'm just a tourist."

Brandy's heard a lot of stories and considers herself hardened but she's touched.

"And is she…?"

Jo looks downcast, shakes her head. Wanting to change the subject, Jo puts on smile.

"What about you, Brandy? Why are you in Paris."

"I love this city and more than anything, I want to report for *Le Figaro*. It's my dream. My father was French and reads it all the time, always a day old. My French is weak and I stumble a lot but the paper has an English desk and I'd give anything to be on it. I'm working on getting an interview. I'm learning more and more French every day. It's the damn verbs I have trouble with, so many variations for the same word. I can write better though. Dear me! For the moment I'm freelancing. I have a travel column in my hometown paper and an advice column under a pseudonym in The Brisbane Record."

Brandy pauses for breath and refreshes her drink from the pitcher. She leans closer, pushes her glasses up. Jo can see the determination on her face.

"I'm working on something big, Jane. I can't say too much right now, other than it's about a prostitution ring. But if I can uncover the story, I'm going to *Le Figaro* with it."

Jo knows firsthand how ruthless pimps can be in protecting their girls, not for their safety but for the pimp's own profit.

"You be careful Brandy. It's a tough world full of greed and decadence. I feel sorry for some of the girls but most get involved willingly."

"Thanks for the warning but I uncovered an unlikely source. The women, girls really, are all underage, kept against their will. But enough about that for now."

She finishes up when both Max and Aurora's attention is turned back to them. Jo has flashes of the children in Thailand that she and an accomplice rescued only a week ago. She knows firsthand the dangers involved and warns Brandy again to be careful. Max sees their almost empty pitcher and brings it to Maurice's attention. Aurora passes Jo a small pipe and a lighter. She points to the washroom door at the end of the bar. Jo looks around, caught off guard at the idea of smoking inside. However, she trusts Aurora and takes it; she needs to pee anyway. Noticing the pipe bowl is full, she smiles at Aurora, who leans closer to her.

"Only one puff, maybe two but no more. Ok?"

"Yeah, yeah. I get it."

Jo attempts to stand. She doesn't realize how good her groove is going and staggers a bit. Her companions notice the shuffle and gentle laughter follows her. Jo manoeuvres through a few clusters of people and bumps into some who smirk at her glassy eyes. She can't remember having this much fun. Trying not to spill the pipe, she cups it in her hand and holds it to her stomach, the lighter in her other hand. She makes it safely to the washroom and talks to herself on the way in.

"Oh, damn, I'm buzzing. No more drinking for me. I'll mellow out with this."

Sitting on the toilet, her jeans at her ankles, she lights up the pipe and takes the shortest of tokes, getting her lungs familiar with what's coming. Then a big one. After exhaling, the cubicle starts to spin. She holds one wall with her free hand until it stops.

"Whoa, settle down. Oh man, it feels good."

She takes another small one and forgetting about the warning, takes another. She taps the pipe out in the bowl between her legs, finishes her toilet and stands up. She has to hang on for a minute; she's having trouble with her balance. Imagine passing out in here with her pants down! She laughs so hard she has to sit back down. By the time she stops, her belly hurts and she can't remember what she was laughing at. At the thought that her friends will wonder what's keeping her, she perks up, gets her blouse tucked back in, sweater straightened and jeans fastened. She overdoes it with soap when she washes her hands. She rinses them off and then finds the hand tissue dispenser is empty. She thinks it funny as well. Drying her hands on her legs, she embarks on a good imitation of someone trying to walk straight.

When she returns to the table, she notices a tall man, long hair in a ponytail, roughly handling Brandy, holding her by the arms. Max is out of his seat, trying to calm the man, who turns to take a swing at Max. Jo may be stoned but she's in tune with her training. Her instincts have been honed by years of confronting aggressive behaviour. The man's eyes are glazed and spittle flies from his lips. Jo steps in and catches his arm in mid-swing. Using the momentum of his motion, she brings down his arm and with a twist, forces it up his back. While she has him in a locked position, she drives her fist into his kidney and he goes to his knees.

The commotion has caused the band to stop playing and people are clamouring, trying to see what's going on. Max, Brandy and Aurora stare at Jo, mouths agape, eyes wide in surprise. Two security people rush to her aid and haul the man off to the back door where they push him into an alley with warnings not to come back or they will call the police. One of them returns to Jo and gives *her a thumbs up* when he sees she's ok. The other one motions for the patrons to carry on, no big deal, trouble over. Brandy is rubbing her arms where the culprit manhandled her.

"Wow, Jane. You're amazing. How did you learn to do that?"

Jo's heart is beating fast, adrenaline flowing. She sits down, panting.

"My dad taught me self-defense when I was younger and I took lessons at a friend's dojang where he teaches Taekwondo. Who was that man?"

"Antoine Basil. I broke up with him a month ago and he can't get over it. He gets violent when he drinks. He never actually hurt me until just now but it was close sometimes. I don't need it in my life even if he is fantastic in bed."

Jo's breathing is back to normal and exhibits a half grin at Brandy's comment. Maurice is wiping the table where sangria has sloshed at the base of an overturned glass. He looks at Jo when he hears Brandy's exclamation of her ex-lover's one good quality. She gets a fuzzy feeling when she thinks of what Maurice might be like in bed. He smiles at her rosy cheeks and shy look.

Things settle down and the incident forgotten with the next batch of drinks. Jo settles for a Pepsi, still reeling with the effects of the pot and the rush of adrenaline. She sits quietly and listens to the music and her friends' chatter. When the band takes a break, Brandy finishes her last glass of wine and decides to change to something stronger. Maurice is busy up front, so she moves through the patrons on her way to the bar. Jo stands to watch her, making sure there are no other threats. Brandy's bidding hello to people she knows, a smile and nod to acquaintances. After she gets her drink she heads for the back, probably the washrooms. Just before she disappears behind the wall by the bandstand, Jo sees an arm reach out and grasp Brandy's forearm to yank her out of sight, toward the back door. Her drink crashes to the floor.

Max and Aurora are startled when Jo sets her drink down roughly on the table and runs toward the hallway. The moving crowd and people dancing in the aisles slow her down. Some of them saw her take down the drunk and get out of her way. She's in time to see the exit door swing shut and but there is no one in the hallway. Rushing toward the door, she bursts through to see a car speed off out the alley. One taillight is broken and when the driver hits the brakes before entering the cross street, she can make out the last two numbers and letters on the plate before it swings on to the street. 64-AF. The streetlights reflect a chrome logo on the trunk, which looks like a lightning bolt to her. The alley is empty. Yellowish lights are sporadic in the opposite direction, a few dumpsters, shadows hiding who knows what. Jo's not getting involved. She needs to tell Max. He'll know what to do. However, she can't get back in. The door is an exit only, so she walks around to the front.

Max and Aurora are standing at one of the upright tables planted on the main floor. Several people are in a group around them and they're pointing and looking in earnest at the back door where Jo disappeared and a waiter is mopping up the sloshed drink and broken glass. Max sees her first and throws up his arms and breaks out in nervous laughter.

"Jane, Jane, what has happened? Where is Brandy?"

"Someone approached her by the back door and pulled her toward the exit. I didn't see who."

She tells them of seeing only the arm and hand of the figure that pulled her away. Aurora gasps, hands to her heart. Max stares at them, stunned.

"It's Antoine Basil, the lowdown…"

"No, no it wasn't him."

"How could you know if you only saw the arm?"

"It was the hand. It had a lot of ink. I couldn't make out the tattoos but there were plenty and Basil didn't have any. This is someone else. When I went out, I saw a car pull away. Brandy wasn't anywhere around. She must've left in the car."

The manager when approached is hesitant about calling the police. Half his clientele will be holding some form of illegal substance and wouldn't fancy a search. He says it's probably the angry boyfriend, regardless of Jo's insistence it's not. Max waves him away with a glare that would boil concrete.

"Come, the Prefecture is not far away."

Max pays his tab and returns to their table to retrieve their coats and leads the women from the bar, disgruntled over the manager's arrogance. When they get outdoors, Jo feels a moment of panic. Her ID will be more closely scrutinized at the station if she has to verify who she is. They're walking at a good pace when they come upon a café and bakery. She has to tell them the truth. She feels her secret will remain a secret with them.

"Hang on you two, I'm still feeling a bit woozy. I'm sorry but I need a couple of minutes. Can we get a coffee? There's something I want to tell you?"

Max and Aurora just look at each other with the same raised brows then follow her in. Max orders an espresso, Aurora water and Jo has tea for a change. Jo insists on paying. They sit at one of the tables in front of the window. A salon curtain gives them some privacy from passersby. She tells them her tale only up to her father's imprisonment and how she helped put him away. Not his suicide. Her travels are to help her forget and in truth to spend her inheritance.

"I need you to trust me when I tell you there are good reasons I travel under another name. I was a police detective for the last five years after being on the force for eight years before that. The most difficult year of my life is behind me but I don't want to be found. I hope you can understand."

At times Jo is an easy read. They can see the hurt in her eyes, the resolve in her speech. Max reaches across the table to take her hand in his.

"Sure Jane, we understand. Or should we call you Jo?"

"Jane will do. That's who I am here. Thank you."

Aurora is speechless. She's never imagined such a tale. When she looks at the woman across the table, she sees a person her mother would call comfortable in their skin.

"What are we going to do about Brandy?"

"That's the reason I'm telling you my story. The police will not pay much attention to our plight. We didn't see any abduction. All I saw was a hand holding her arm, then a vehicle speeding away. While it looks suspicious to us, it won't to them. We don't know who it is. We don't know anything at this point. She may have gone willingly."

Aurora looks at Jo defiantly, not comfortable with what she's saying.

"She would've said goodbye, don't you think, Max?"

21

"She's done it before Aurora. Met someone, got carried away and left without telling us. We always hear from her the next day. Maybe Jane's right. What should we do, Jane?"

"I think we need to have a closer look right now. Search for some clues and then decide what to do. Do you know where we can get our hands on some flashlights?"

Max gets up.

"Be right back."

He's only gone ten minutes and returns with a plastic bag swinging from his hand. Joining the ladies again, he removes three small plastic flashlights from the bag, gives one each to Jo and Aurora and puts the third one in his jacket pocket.

"Got these at the all-night convenience store up the street. Let's go."

The three of them are in the alley behind the bar. Jo gets Max to walk one side from the corner to the bar and Aurora the other, while Jo sweeps the middle. Aurora is poking at the edge of the building, probing small clusters of weeds.

"What are we looking for?"

"Anything out of the ordinary. Something which fell recently, not buried under weeds or debris."

The three sleuths walk slowly toward the club door, sweeping their lights back and forth in a pendulum, stopping occasionally to pick at something on the ground that looks suspect. When Jo reaches a spot close to the back door, something glints in the light. Waving the flashlight closer to the ground, she sees something odd.

"I found something."

CHAPTER 4

Max and Aurora gather around her and watch as she bends down to pick up a pair of tortoiseshell glasses from a clump of weeds. Aurora takes them in her hand.

"These are Brandy's. She bought them only a week ago."

"Yes, they look like the ones she was wearing earlier," Jo says.

Jo and Max are inspecting the ground closer to where the glasses were. Jo sees scuff marks on the cobblestones, fresh scratch marks from tiny loose stones.

"Looks like a scuffle took place right here. I don't think Brandy got in the car willingly. We can assume she was abducted but this isn't much to go on. She could've dropped the glasses without realizing it and the marks on the street might not have been from that particular time. I saw other people leaving by the back during the evening."

Max continues to search the ground around the alleyway where the car may have been sitting. Little tufts of slender grasses and tangled weeds have grown between some of the cobblestones where they've come loose over the years. Some are squashed down where a car has driven over them, or people walked on them, but many stick up like punk haircuts. Max moves some of them around with his foot. In one of them near the abrasions on the stone, he knocks a loose piece of paper clear. It's the size of a book of paper matches.

"Hey, look here."

He passes it to Jo and holds his light so she can see. It's folded several times, and when Jo unfolds it, they can see the creases are weak and thin as if it's been opened and re-folded many times. Before they can read it, they have to move aside to make way for an auto creeping slowly toward them. It stops three or four car lengths away. Everyone waits, the three staring at the headlights, whoever is in the car staring at them. A minute of quiet goes by before Max waves angrily at the car to carry on. It doesn't move. Max is about to approach it when the vehicle slowly moves forward and he hustles back to the ladies between Jo and Aurora.

When the car comes abreast of them, it stops. The windows are heavily shaded. The one in the front descends to halfway. All they see is the top of a head. In the dark it's difficult to distinguish any features but they can easily see the barrel of a shotgun aimed at them. A gravelly voice from inside threatens them.

"Give us that paper and you can all walk away. Otherwise, your insides will be all over the wall behind you. Your choice."

His command is in French and Max has to translate. Jo has to step forward carefully with the paper in her raised hand. She records everything she can - a long haired person, the fruity smell of disinfectant. A glint of light from an open door up the street exposes the face for mere seconds. Before he moves away, she sees a tattoo on his forehead. The hand that reached through the window and takes the paper also has heavy ink. Both the paper and the shotgun disappear in a flash and the car squeals away. It almost causes an accident when it pulls onto the street without stopping. Jo turns around to face her partners and Aurora faints.

The excitement is too much for Aurora. When she arrives back to her apartment a half hour later, she falls into bed. Max and Jo drink coffee at one o'clock in the morning, discussing what happened in the alley. Max has his hands wrapped around his mug, sitting close to the dining room table. He has to hold it tight to stop his hands from shaking.

"You okay, Max?"

"*Non*. I'm not okay, Jane. I don't usually have to stare at the barrel of a threatening gun when I entertain friends. What was that all about? What has this got to do with Brandy?"

"The only thing I can think of is that Brandy confided to me earlier that she was working on a story to expose a prostitution ring here in the city. She was hoping to build a story for Le Figaro where she wanted to find a position."

Max sits up straight, surprise on his face.

"A prostitution ring? There are prostitutes everywhere in this city. What can be so newsworthy about that?"

Jo stares at the floor for a moment, lost in a memory. The young girls she helped were likely destined for the same fate. She still gets a flush of anger when she thinks of what she just went through in Thailand, hoping that it's not the same thing. She's not sure she can handle more missing children.

"I think this has something to do with young women being held against their will."

"*Merde.* Now what Jane? Don't you think we have enough now to go to the police?"

"Here's what we do have Max. The car was the same one that took Brandy, I saw the plate and it's the same as I saw before. The digits 64-AF were clearly visible and now I know the rest, DD-164-AF. According to your registration plates, doesn't this point out the region it is from? And a logo I thought was a lightning bolt is actually the Hyundai logo. I know this is the same vehicle."

"Yes, it the plate does show the region. The police can use that."

"Maybe we can, too. And another thing. The hand with the gun, I believe it is the same hand I saw grab Brandy's arm, and I saw a tattoo on the forehead, an upside down cross with a snake wrapped around it, almost like a caduceus. That ring any bells?"

"I'm not sure of the word *caduceus*?"

"I don't know the French word but hang on a minute."

Jo gets up and searches around the kitchen for something to write on. Noticing a small notepad and pencil by the phone, she grabs it and draws first a rough caduceus and then the upside down cross she saw. Pointing to the first one, she turns the page so Max can see it.

"Ah, *oui*, the medical symbol. And yes, I recognize the upside down one now. It's a symbol for a biker gang called La Croix de Mise à Mort or The Killing Cross. People call them La Croix. I don't know what it signifies but they've been linked to anti-church activities, disrupting services and masses, destroying religious icons and buildings. I expect they're into drugs and other illegal practices."

"Do you know where they hang out?"

"No, I don't."

He's quiet and Jo can see he's thinking. She's debating how much more she should get involved. She wants peace and quiet in her life but the cop side of her can't turn away from what's happening. In fact, it sparks something in her. The need to know. The idea of putting bad people away gives her a rush similar to a puff on the pipe. Maybe she can help. Her thoughts are interrupted when Max slides his chair back and refills his cup. He offers her some but she waves him away.

"What are you thinking Max?"

"I might know someone who can help us with the bikers. Wish we could've seen what was on that paper."

"I did see a little. There was a bunch of numbers and on the bottom was the word, Cicero."

Max's eyes go wide with the mention of that name. He almost drops the coffee pot.

"Are you sure that's what you saw, Jane?"

"Pretty sure."

"Cicero is a rumour. The name is associated with some gruesome crimes. Sickens me to talk about it. From what I understand, it's part of the French Mob, our organized crime element. I don't know a lot, but enough to know that name is not good news. Maybe we should go to the police."

"Maybe we should. We're running short on time. They took her over two hours ago. There must be something we have to find a trail. Who's this person you know?"

Max goes to the sink and leaves his cup on the sideboard. He holds his back and stretches backwards with a grimace on his face.

"Oh, these old bones. I know you had a sleep earlier. I need some rest, my dear. Give me a minute."

Max takes out his cell phone and wanders into the living room, speaking low. Silence. Then laughter. He comes back to the dining room with a weak smile.

"When you go out the front door, turn left to Rue Brule. After two blocks there is a café and bakery, *Le Hibou Sage*. It's opened all night. A man will meet you there shortly if you are keen."

Jo perks up. Some sleuthing to do. She's not a bit tired.

"Perfect, and this gentleman's name?"

"Bertrand Poitras. And he's no gentleman. A bit shifty but he and I go way back. I spoke quite highly of you so naturally he's curious, and he knows a thing or two about the *Lagrange* family."

"The *Lagrange* family?"

"*Oui*, from where the rumour of Cicero emanates. Now off with you. Check in with me in a couple of hours. That's all I need. We'll decide then what to do. I doubt we'll see Aurora until tomorrow, late riser as she is. *Bonsoir.*"

"Wait, Max. What was so funny?"

"I described you to him so he would know who to look for. He'd agreed to go on my promise that you were beautiful."

Jo's red-cheeked when Max disappears up the stairway. Donning her boots and jacket, she pulls on her toque as she leaves. The café is only five minutes away. The street is active even at this time of night but in a lazy, slow-motion kind of way, inhabited with stragglers, late night workers, revelers, or criminals. Every big city is the same. It never really shuts down. You can always find its pulse. Few people are on the sidewalk, only a couple hand in hand strolling away from her and a clutch of adolescents on the opposite corner. Laughter, smoke and girlish shrieks ascend from the cluster until they move off the other way. Jo enters a brightly lit, welcoming atmosphere, filled with a comforting hum of easy conversation, and scents of sugared treats and coffee perking in the air.

She looks around, not seeing any man waiting or beckoning to her. He probably won't be long. The aroma of fresh bread causes her to pause and breathe it in. It's her favourite scent. It reminds her of her mother who once made bread every week. There are about a dozen round tables with chairs on the right and toward the back. A counter is on the left, cradled between two slanted glass showcases with a display of mouthwatering delicacies. A young lady is being served, about to join three others at one of the four tables occupied.

Jo steps up to the counter, removing her gloves and hat. She brings her hand gently through her hair to let loose her curls. As she hasn't eaten much in a while, she has an urge to eat everything behind the glass. Using her best high school French, she orders something to drink and two croissants. What she receives is her coffee with two milk and two pickles on a plate. Seeing the sour look on Jo's face as she stares at the pickles, the young server has an impish grin and asks Jo in broken English.

"You no want pickle?"

Jo shakes her head, her lips tightly sealed. She doesn't want to start laughing at herself. The young girl matches her head movements, sets the plate aside and raises her hand palm side up. Jo points at the croissants with the chocolate on them and offers two fingers. The server hands Jo back her change after she pays but Jo waves it away. The girl offers her the pickles and they both start laughing.

"You want? How you say, over the house."

"On the house."

"*Oui, oui*, on the house. You want?"

Jo has the munchies and the pickles don't look bad, long dills and she can smell the garlic and vinegar, maybe even a hint of wine. She'll eat those first.

"Yes. *Oui, merci.*"

Balancing the coffee, the plate with the croissants, her toque and gloves and the pickles, she takes a seat halfway back on the opposite side of the others, toward the kitchen and hanging her coat on the back of a chair. Jo wishes she'd brought a change of clothes. She freshened up before they went out but she's starting to feel a little rough around the edges. She'll do what she can and if nothing bears fruit by morning, they'll go to the police.

She's starting on her first pastry after finishing the pickles when she spies a tall, dark man enter the café. He's bundled up in a navy pea jacket with a grey and blue paisley scarf around his neck. His hair is long, slicked back behind his ears with a few streaks of grey to add to the proverbial distinction. He swaggers like a man who deems his presence important. The goatee reminds Jo of her former partner, Adam Thorne. He had a goatee for a short while but his wife hated it. Jo had liked it.

The stranger waves and blows kisses to two older ladies at one of the tables. He glances toward Jo and recognizing her, waves a pointed finger and smiles. Jo's heart does a flip flop. He's incredibly handsome. She waves back with a tightlipped smile, feeling a little foolish. She pays attention to her croissant. But out of the corner of her eye, she watches him.

While undoing his coat, he banters with the attendant. She grins at his comments, whatever they are, and stares at him with a face that says I've-heard-it-all. When she slides him his coffee and pastry, he bends over the counter to peck the lady on the cheek. She pushes him away and the two are laughing as he struts toward Jo.

"Bonsoir, Jane. Ah, give me one moment."

He places his cup and plate down, slips off the jacket and hangs it on a vacant chair. Jo is looking at him with a curious look. He steps up to her, takes her hand and plants a soft kiss upon it.

"Welcome to *Gay Paris*. It truly is a pleasure to meet you Jane Taylor. Our friend, Max, did not let me down. You are indeed beautiful."

Jo looks away amused at the man's candour. She's heard a lot of bullshit in her life but this guy's good. She loves it.

"Thank you but you're too kind. Glad to meet you. I apologize for Max disturbing you so late in the night. But it's extremely important. Do you know Brandy?"

"Not personally. Only through Max. Tell me what's going on."

Jo tells him what she knows, trusting him because of Max. The man seems genuinely concerned and interrupts if something is not clear.

"So, we have the paper, the tattooed hand, the biker's involvement, the make and plate of the car... you have the plate digits and what kind it was?"

"I do."

Reaching over to dig into his jacket pocket he removes a notebook and a stub of a pencil. The notebook is well used with half the pages puffed with usage and many entries.

"What are they?"

"DD-164-AF. A Hyundai, dark blue or black, don't know what model."

"Give me a minute."

In another pocket he takes out his smartphone. He hits the phone icon, then Contacts and scrolls down to *Emile au travail* (Emile at work). Jo's thinking of the smooth rhythm of the French Language, the rolling of the letter R especially appealing. She can't stop staring at his eyes. She can't remember ever seeing anyone having such a penetrating deep brown, softened with a mischievous glint.

"Allo Emile, mon ami. It's Bert calling. Can you talk?"

"Oui. I'm doing a stake-out and it's quiet. Partner's walking the street."

"I've got you down for twenty euros on this weekend's game between the Boxers and the Dragons with the Dragons taking it by two points or more. Pays ten to one. That right?"

"Glad you called. Up it to forty."

"Hey, listen my friend. You're already into me for two hundred. You need to pay up soon."

"I know, I know. It's these crazy shifts, man. You know I'm good for it. I've always paid my tab with you, Bert. You know that."

"Yeah, yeah. Ok. Forty then. Listen, I need a favour. You got your fancy little computer there in your car? Run a plate for me, will you?"

A pause from the gendarme. "What's going on Bert?"

"It's nothing really but you know, I saw a super-hot chick, man, in this Hyundai. She waved but I can't remember her... but I'd like to. You know what I mean Emile? C'mon, it'll only take you a minute."

"Just this once, what is it?"

Bertrand gives him the plate numbers and closes off after Emile says he'll call him back.

Placing the phone on the table, he replaces it with his coffee and tells Jo who his contact is and the small gaming gig he has going on. She doesn't like the cop connection with a bookie but it's not the worst thing in the world. Bertrand doesn't look big time to her. Probably a close ring of a couple hundred subscribers. She's dealt with his kind before. Totally harmless but illegal. Jo and her associates back in Canada turned a blind eye to the small enterprises due to their incredible wealth of gossip and dirt that could be used for twisting a few arms.

"Now we can wait so I'll refill our coffees if you like, and I'll tell you about the Lagrange family and the bikers."

Jo offers up her mug.

"Just black, please."

When he returns, he asks Jo directly.

"What's your involvement in this? Who are you? Max vouched for you and that's good enough for me but..."

He offers the statement with both hands palms up.

"I want to help. I have experience looking for people. I trust Max too or I wouldn't take up your time."

"Experience? How so?"

He's met with a stony glare, no comment. He shrugs and sits forward.

"Fine. Now here's what I'm hearing. The Lagrange family is the brains with the money, the Killing Cross merely sycophants doing the bidding of their overlord, Felix Lagrange. Mules most likely, moving drugs and smuggling. Practising strong arm intimidation and revenge. And from what you told me, obviously kidnapping. Half of them are dumber than a doughnut. Their loyalty and services are rewarded with drugs."

Jo pushes her cup aside and folds her hands in front of her, elbows on the table.

"Are they killers?"

Bertrand shrugs with tightened lips.

"Probably, but nothing's ever been pinned on them. I mean they're lowlife. They're capable of anything. Your friend must've found a leak and they were told to tap it. Maybe she'll just be threatened. I don't know what they'll do."

"Do you have any idea where they hang their hats, where they park their bikes?"

"I hear rumours, nothing solid because I had no reason, or desire, to verify it. They're said to occupy an old farmhouse about twenty kilometers or so outside the city. Not sure where. The main… "

He's interrupted by the vibration of his phone. Checking the screen, he holds up a finger to Jo.

"It's Emile. Hey there, what do you have for me?"

Bertrand listens, nodding occasionally. He sits up suddenly with his face scrunched up and ends the call with a frown.

"*Merci, mon ami.*"

"The vehicle is registered to Dietrich Achthoven, a petty crook. Mother's French. Father's Dutch, obviously. Forty-one years old. Did time for assault with a deadly weapon. Nothing on his record for the last two years. An address in Les Coudrées, a few kilos north of Sartrouville. There are still rural areas around there, some farms, crops and cattle. Might be a good place to start our search."

"Our search?"

"*Bien oui.* You think I'm going to let you run off and have all the fun. It is my chance to be a hero and rescue a damsel in distress. And besides, you don't look that tough. You need a bodyguard and I just happen to be free, even if it is the middle of the night. I have a vehicle not far from here."

Jo straightens her shoulders and sticks out her chin. She eyes him suspiciously as she ponders his suggestion.

"Don't worry about me, hero. I'm a bit tougher than you think. I may have to be your bodyguard."

He snickers at her offer and starts to put his coat on.

"Let's go. My place is a ten-minute walk. We'll get the car. Sartrouville is about a half hour away."

Jo bundles up again and follows her new partner. She's warming up to him. He seems genuine but she worries whether or not he can handle himself.

"If we run into some bad guys Bertrand, do I have to babysit you?"

He's just a step ahead of her, leading her into an alley that runs at the rear of abutting buildings.

"Welterweight champion at university level, spar for a hobby and exercise at Catelli's Gym. I'm fine. You watch my back and I'll watch yours. Deal?"

"Deal. Now what are you looking for?"

"We're almost there."

Another three driveways and at the rear of a three-storey stone building is a BMW X3. The rich lines defined in the low light of the streetlamps, and the red glint of its taillights, gives a it feral look. He pushes a button on his key, makes it bleep and tells her to jump in. Another button starts the car.

"I'll be right back."

Jo watches him unlock a back door and when he flips on a light switch, she sees him ascend a flight of stairs. He's only gone a few moments before returning with something in his hand. As he comes closer, Jo can see the end of a baseball bat he is pounding in his palm. With an impish grin on his face, he opens the driver's door and chucks the bat behind the seat.

"A little protection if things get out of hand. Or as a persuader, if you know what I mean?"

"You just happened to have a bat?"

He's quiet as he backs the car out into the narrow alley. The car lights flash on garbage bins, short fences and open driveways until they turn onto a thoroughfare. It's only when they are on the main artery northwest out of the city does he speak.

"It was my son's. He died in a car accident when he was ten. That was eight years ago. My marriage dissolved after. I keep the bat for sentimental reasons. He loved baseball. I still have his glove, too."

"I'm sorry, Bertrand."

"Nothing to be sorry for. It's been a long time and I'm learning to live with the memories. And besides, it'll be handy if I need to crack a few skulls. Now let's check this Dietrich fellow out."

32

CHAPTER 5

They take highway D908 until he hits Avenue Gabriel Peri. He lights a cigarette but when he sees Jo's face squished up, he tosses it out the window.

"You don't smoke?"

"Tried it once but I don't care for the smell."

They drive off the street to a narrower, darker one. Two clicks from the centre of Sartrouville is a collection of run-down houses, grouped around a circular court. Checking the address, they find the house abandoned with boards nailed over the windows and doors. None of the cars parked nearby is a Hyundai. Bertrand slowly moves away but Jo sits up and peers closer through the windshield.

"Hold on. Bertrand. Look on the left side of the house. There's a path there. Looks like a lot of traffic going to the rear. Kill your lights. I want to look to see if anyone's around."

The house next to this one is boarded up as well. Of the two facing, one has lights on in the rear and the other remains dark. There's no movement anywhere. Bertrand does a U-turn in the circular street and parks the car several houses away under a broken streetlamp. Darkness covers their movements. He brings his bat. They cross the street and skitter in behind the darkened house next to the one they assume is Achthoven's. Scrub brush, busted garbage bags, a broken bicycle and old boards make walking tricky. The only light is from streetlights on the court adjacent to the one they are on. Jo almost trips but Bertrand grabs hold of her with his free hand, almost dropping the bat. He admonishes her in a whisper.

"Careful there, Jane."

Jo gets a rush from the strong arm holding her and the musky scent of his cologne. She clears her throat and moves away. Their eyes meet in the semi-darkness and Jo's heart beats a little faster. She's embarrassed by what's crossing her mind.

"Thanks for catching me."

All he thinks of is how her slender body fit next to him when he pulled her back from falling. He smiles to himself.

"Yes, well, there's not much light. It's easy to trip over this junk."

They make their way to the edge of the house and can see behind Achthoven's place. The worn path leads to a large garage. Tall trees and thick bushes form a natural wall around the building. Anyone would be hard put to make it out from the street or from behind. The house is a storey and a half with a high peaked roof. The outline of a door on the side is visible. A larger door on the front looks eerie with blotches of paint peeling from the metal. Moving closer to the side door, they can see a large padlock the size of a man's fist hanging from a catch. Jo speaks low.

"That's one tough looking lock."

"*Oui*, it is. But look there, Jane."

Bertrand is pointing to a basement window only visible in the rear of the house where a light flickers from within. Forgetting the garage, Jo creeps to the window and kneels so she can peek in. The stillness of the night is broken by her loud gasp. She recoils from the view and falls on her rump. Bertrand bends to help her up and sees what she saw.

Brandy Williams is suspended from a floor joist by a thick rope tying her wrists together. Her toes barely touch the dirty concrete floor. Her head hangs down, her forehead crusty with blood. Her upper body is naked. Cut marks across her breasts and stomach smirk at them with crimson lips. Blood has run from the wounds and looks like dripping paint. Jo covers her mouth and tears roll down from her eyes as she gathers enough courage to look back. She's seen worse but not on someone she only met hours ago. It stings. Wiping her eyes with the back of her hand, her shock turns to anger. She curses the men who've done this.

"Bastards. We need to get her out of there. I hope she's not dead."

Bertrand tries to see more. He moves close to the window and wipes off some of the grit.

"I think I see her chest moving. She's still alive. Wait, look just beyond her, to the right."

Jo stays low and peers in. A body is sprawled out on a decrepit couch in the back corner of the room. They can't see the face, only the outline of a prone person, but the long frame and heavy boots suggest a man. A battered coffee table sits in front of him. Half a dozen candles burn at one edge. Empty beer bottles, an overflowing ashtray, a hookah and a sawed-off shotgun litter the rest. The man rouses and turns over, one hand coming to rest near the floor and flopping off the edge of the couch. Multiple tattoos are visible in the wavering light. Jo and Bertrand jump back. Sitting on the cold ground next to each other, Bertrand can feel Jo shaking.

"What now?"

"Let me think. We don't know if anyone else is in there."

She looks around while she contemplates their next move. She instructs Bertrand on what he can do.

"Sneak up the back steps beside us and see if the door is locked. Be careful and be quiet. I'll watch the jerk in the basement."

He rises and hustles the four feet to the bottom of three steps that lead up to an eight-foot-wide covered stoop. One of the boards creaks and he freezes. He looks at Jo and she waves him on when she sees no movement. Bertrand steps closer, grabs the doorknob and turns it, finding the door unlocked. Avoiding the loose board, he rushes back to Jo's side.

"It's open. Should we go in?"

"That was my first thought but we don't know who else is in there. I doubt he's alone. Let me think for a minute."

She checks her surroundings, looking for some kind of diversion.

"Ok, here's what we'll we do."

Jo hurries over to the far right of the garage where she saw a pile of garbage bags. There might be something in there she can use. The top bag has a tear in it and an old newspaper lies crumpled on the top. She has to enlarge the hole to pull out several other sheets of newsprint. Two old milk cartons, the kind with the waxy surface, lie underneath the newspaper and she brings them too. She snaps a bunch of dry twigs off the end of branches on a nearby tree. Returning to where Bertrand waits at the foot of the steps, she whispers.

"Give me your lighter."

He hands it to her.

"What are you planning?"

"I'm going to build a fire in front of the window and when it's burning bright enough, I'll bang on it. The man will see the flames and hopefully be disoriented. He will likely run out to see what's going on and if there is anyone else, they might too. I want you to get by the door on the side it opens with your bat. Wait for a moment to see if more than one comes out. If so, let the first ones go to the fire and take the last man down."

"What will you be doing?"

"I'll be waiting around the side where I can see whoever tries to put out the fire."

He sees that she's barehanded, her gloves missing.

"With what?"

She holds up her hands, curled into fists.

"With these and my bad temper."

Being a tad macho, Bertrand normally might laugh at someone as lithe as Jo depending on her fists but he can feel her wrath.

"Whatever you say but be careful. What if there's more than two?"

She doesn't answer because she doesn't know. She starts to crinkle the newspaper in wads, propping them tightly by sticking the branches close like a tiny tepee around the drier and smaller twigs directly on top, then balancing the two milk cartons on top of each other. Using the lighter she sets the tiny flame to the edge of the paper. It flares up right away. She waits until the milk cartons catch. When the flames rise up into the window, she whacks on the glass.

The tattooed man wakes with a start, looking around as if he doesn't know where he is. When he sees the flames, he shouts something Jo hears but can't understand. A light goes on in a window in the back room on the top level. It's covered and offers little light to the back yard.

Less than thirty seconds go by before a bearded man, heavy in gut, dressed in T-shirt, Daffy Duck lounging pants and unlaced work boots, barrels from the back door, his attention on the flames. He's cursing and looking for the culprits as he goes to stamp out the flames. Not far behind him comes the tattooed man, brandishing the shotgun. He stops at the head of the stairs to watch his companion stomp out the flames, and eyes the shadows.

Bertrand waits ten seconds and when there is no one else, he steps out and with bottled rage and a practiced swing, hits Mr. Ink mid-thigh, crashing him to the floor. The gun clatters down the steps. The scream of pain alerts the tattooed man. Even Jo hears the bone break. The fallen man doesn't have the chance to scream again when Bertrand kicks him on the head, not caring if he kills him.

In the few seconds it takes the tattooed man to react, Jo steps out. With a hardened fist, she hits him in the left temple. He staggers from the punch. It's not powerful enough to render him unconscious but he falls to his knees facing Jo. She steps forward with intention of kicking the man in the solar plexus but he recovers enough to see the foot coming. Grabbing it, he flips Jo over with the momentum of her kick.

Jo falls. Her head disturbs the dying fire causing sparks fly in the air, on her face and in her hair. More concerned about the hot embers, she's not prepared for big man's kick. He catches her in the chest. But he's off balance, and the kick is weak. Jo recoils from the impact and springs to her feet. Before he can counteract, she delivers a round-house kick to his head, and he's down. Balancing herself to strike if he moves, she's interrupted by Bertrand laughing.

"And I was worried about you."

"Except for these burn marks on my cheek and the singed hair, I'm fine. You?"

"No problem here. The bat works great."

"See if you can find something to tie them up with. I'll go get Brandy."

"Shouldn't we call the gendarme?"

"Yes. After we leave."

She hastens into the house and is disoriented until she sees an open door in a short hallway between the kitchen and the front entrance. She takes the stairs to the basement two at a time and finds Brandy. Jo is flushed from the adrenaline rush but the sight of the poor woman almost bowls her over. The cuts are not as deep as she thought. The brittle blood looks like red worms on the lip of the wounds. She clips the woman free using a utility knife she finds on the floor by a work-bench. Jo catches Brandy before her head hits the concrete. Laying her down gently, Jo removes her jacket and puts it on the half-naked woman. The movement stirs Brandy and with one eye, she focuses on her rescuer. Her voice is strained and weak.

"Jane? Is that you, Jane? Oh, it hurts so much."

"It's me. Now I need you to be tough. We need to get you out of here, and I can't carry you."

Even with Jo's help it takes an extreme effort for Brandy to stand. Her arms are useless. Her face is puffy with one eye swollen shut. Jo waits until Brandy gets her legs and steers her up the stairs. When they reach the back stoop, they discover Bertrand tying knots to the tattooed man's wrists. He's not going anywhere on those legs. The other man is lying face down on the stoop, still unconscious. Jo nods her approval.

"Perfect. Let's go. As soon as we're away, call your friend Emile."

He helps Jo steady Brandy and together they get her down the driveway with as much haste as she can bear.

"Not Emile on this one. I think an emergency call will work. I don't want any connection to this."

Jo looks over Brandy's shoulder at him with a weak smile. "Might be too late for that."

CHAPTER 6

Brandy is lying in the back seat with a blanket from the trunk wrapped around her. Jo has replaced her jacket and shakes her head at the blood stains she knows she won't get off. They are back on Avenue Gabriel Peri. Bertrand is zooming southwest toward the city, ignoring the speed limit.

"There's a hospital not far from here."

"No hospital, please Bertrand. Her wounds look superficial. Let's get her to Aurora's place and we'll get her patched up, at least until she and Max can get Brandy to a hospital."

Bertrand looks at her with a rutted brow.

"Why not, Jane? You can see she's been knocked about the head. She may have a concussion."

"I didn't detect any signs of a concussion although I can't rule it out. I'm not a doctor but I've been around other beatings, and she's coherent and her speech was not slurred. There's another reason."

He looks askance at her with wide eyes showing his surprise.

"And what would that be?"

She stares at him for a moment, trying to decide if she can trust him. He questions her silence with an open palm and a questioning look.

"My name's not Jane."

By the time they reach Aurora's apartment, she's explained her dilemma and asks his forbearance. He's been silent the whole time. A soft moan from the back seat disturbs them. Brandy's now waking out of a deep sleep. Bertrand points to Aurora's front door.

"Let's get her inside. Go knock on the door. I expect Max will be waiting for us even though it's almost dawn. He's likely to be pacing the living room worrying about us if I know Max. I'll get Brandy on her feet and inside."

Jo is almost to the door when Max and Aurora burst out onto the street. Aurora gasps, hands over her mouth, at the sight of Brandy. Max goes glassy eyed and rushes to help Bertrand. They get Brandy upstairs, still with the blanket wrapped around her shoulders and upper body. She refuses to lie down. They sit her at the kitchen table where she rests her elbows on the top and holds her head, trying not to cry. She's thirsty and sore everywhere and calls for a drink of water and painkillers, whatever Aurora has. Aurora rushes to the medicine cabinet in the downstairs bathroom. Max runs the tap to get the water cold. Bertrand sits at the side of the table, remaining quiet as Jo brushes the hair from Brandy's face to examine her wounds.

There is a cut on the upper lip. A puffy eye turning bluish black. The nose has bled, leaving crusty trails on her chin and left cheek. Jo turns to Aurora when she returns with two white pills, which she hesitates to pass to Brandy.

"Are you allergic to Acetaminophen? Aspirin? I don't have anything stronger."

Brandy shakes her head and reaches out for them with a trembling hand. Max passes her the glass of water but Brandy's shaking too much to hold the glass. Jo takes it and after Brandy pops the pills in her mouth, Jo holds the glass to her quivering lips. Jo then turns to Aurora.

"Do you have a first aid kit with bandages and plasters? And a bowl with warm water and a cloth?"

Aurora moves into action pointing to cupboard near the dishwasher in the kitchen.

"Max, grab a large bowl from the cabinet and fill it for Jo. I've got plasters and ointment for the cuts."

Jo shakes her head.

"It gets worse, Aurora. She has cuts to her body too but they're not deep. Let's get her into the washroom to clean her up. You guys will have to leave us alone for a few minutes. Bertrand, go call the police on a nearby pay phone."

Aurora returns with a small woven basket with a removable top. It's filled with bandages, different size plasters and a tube of antiseptic cream. Jo digs through it quickly.

"Max, we're going to need larger plasters, maybe two inches by four or five. Is there an all-night pharmacy close by? I know back in Canada we can buy them in a roll."

"Yes, two streets over. How many do you need?"

"At least a half a dozen or a full roll. Thanks, Max."

He grabs his jacket and leaves. Bertrand goes with him. The ladies get Brandy up and usher her to the bathroom where Aurora had already started a bath running. They get her inside, chuck the blanket back into the hallway and undress her. After wiping away the blood and reassuring themselves that none of the cuts requires stitches, they help her settle into the tepid water. A small shriek emits from Brandy's lips when the water contacts the wounds. Gritting her teeth, she settles down and with closed eyes, a heavy sigh signals her relief.

When the dawn turns the darkness to grey, Brandy is asleep upstairs in the guest room. Several cuts to the body required the large plasters. All wounds have been dressed and antiseptic properly applied. A cold pack to her eye has reduced the swelling. Max is toasting bagels for everyone. Aurora makes fresh coffee and when they are seated, she retrieves a pint of brandy from the cupboard over the stove and before sitting down. She adds a generous portion to hers and offers it to the others. They all take her up on it.

"Oh dear, the poor woman. How could people do this to my friend? From the bottom of my heart, thank you both, Bertrand and Jane… or do we call you Jo?"

Jo wipes her mouth with her napkin and drops it on her lap. She offers a half-hearted smile.

"I think I'll stick with Jane. Safer for me if people are looking this way. I just need to stay off the radar."

"Our lips are sealed, *ma cherie*. Do not worry. We are indebted to you. Now tell us what happened."

Jo and Bertrand tell them of their contact with his cop friend. The plate number. The old house and their suspicions. Finding Brandy. Here Aurora holds a napkin to her lips and a tear stains the top fold. Max shakes his head with an angry face. Taking a break from conversation, they finish their bagels. During second coffees and more brandy, Bertrand relates Jo's clever plan to gain the bad guys' attention. Jo eyes Bertrand with an affectionate twinkle when she tells them of him stepping up to their defense. He in turn slices the air with a few faux karate chops and lightens the mood, suggesting in jest that Jo might need a bodyguard. Then she tells of their arrival here. Max sits forward, forearms on the table, one fist balled up in the other, in a grinding motion.

"I'm glad to hear you gave them a taste of their own monstrous ways. Now what?"

Thinking of the authorities makes Jo reluctant to get more involved. They got Brandy back. Perhaps she should step away from this and head south, maybe Nice. But her gut and instinct tell her she can't. Brandy is still in danger. Whoever those ruffians worked for is going to be extremely upset. Jo goes over the scenario of what will happen when the police arrive. What would she do? The answer to that question hangs on whether she's the first one there, or after the scene has been secured. Regardless, something identifying Brandy is sure to be there. In Jo's hasty retreat, she didn't see any clothing in the basement, nor was she thinking of the small bag that she remembers Brandy wore over her shoulder. They have to be in the house somewhere. She explains her thoughts to the others.

"The police will be involved one way or the other soon enough. They'll have picked up the culprits by now and I'm sure they'll be in detention at the nearest lock-up. If they're part of the biker gang, they'll likely have lawyers for them soon. At least in Canada they would. This Cicero connection bothers me."

She pauses for a moment, hating to state the obvious.

"And they'll be looking for Brandy. She's not out of danger. These ruffians we subdued are low life on the bottom of the malicious pile. Whoever orchestrated the kidnapping and torture would not want her to remain alive, whether she told them everything or nothing. They will be hunting for her. I'm thinking we let the police handle it and I should step out of the picture so…"

"*Non!*"

They're all startled by Max's outburst. He slaps his open hand on the table rattling the coffee cups.

"You can't leave us now Jane. We need to know why this happened so we can put an end to the matter. If like you say she is still in danger, then it's up to us her friends to protect her. You and Bertrand, brave hearts, got her back. Help us keep her."

Aurora is aggressively nodding during Max's plea.

"I agree. Please help us Jane."

Bertrand shrugs with his hands up, there's nothing else he can add, but his look tells her he wishes she'd stay.

"Ok. But you people deal with the police."

They are all smiles, shoulders relaxed. Max repeats what each one is thinking.

"What should we do now?"

"I'd like to take another look at the alley. Walk it one more time. Maybe I missed something. The piece of paper they dropped was important enough for them to come back looking for it and threaten us with a gun to get it back. It bothers me."

Jo pushes her chair away from the table and stands, stretching her arms out and straightening her back.

"Right now, I need to lie down. I need some sleep. We all do I'm sure. I expect neither you, Max, nor Aurora got much either. You were both up when we got back. You too, Bertrand. So Aurora, where can I lie down, please?"

Aurora has also risen and stares at the couch in the living room, which is more the size of love seat rather than a full length.

"You'll have to curl up, Jane. I'll get you a blanket and sheets."

Bertrand has already made his way to the front door, zipping up his jacket.

"I have space at my apartment, Jane. There's an extra bed. You're welcome to stretch out there and we can all meet back here at…" Checks his wrist. "… say eleven? It's a little after six now."

"Can we say noon? I need to do some shopping. I'd like to run by the alley near the bar again, see if we missed anything, any clues. I can't stop thinking of the folded paper that was important enough for them to threaten us. It looked like it had only numbers on it. Plus I didn't bring a change of clothes. Nor make-up as you can see. Max said we'd only be gone for the day."

She raises her brows at Max with a delicate smirk. He gets a chuckle from her quip. She's glad her hair is short, her curls falling naturally without brushing. She knows she's probably a mess even though she doesn't normally wear a lot of cosmetics. Bertrand is staring at her with interest.

"I think you look fine."

Jo's cheeks glow like soft embers and she looks away. Max winks at Aurora and she interrupts the shy encounter.

"Get going then and yes, I too am tired. I expect Brandy will sleep for a while. Come Max, you can tuck me in."

Now Jo winks at Max who grins like he just won a prize.

CHAPTER 7

Bertrand drives the short distance to his place and they remain silent, each in their own thoughts. Jo finds her feelings toward him unsettling. It's been a long time since she enjoyed the comforts of a lover's arm around her. She was always caught up in her work, doing crazy hours and never found the right man that wasn't jealous of her career. She gave up after her last boyfriend. Now it seems so long ago that she can't remember. She feels his eyes on her. When she turns to look at him, he returns his eyes to the road. She likes his strong silhouette.

Bertrand is thinking similar thoughts. He gets a giddy feeling when they are close. He loves the mysterious look in her eyes, the confidence she exudes when making decisions. He likes her independence and free spirit. At least, it is how he sees her. Plus, she's got a hot body. The physical attraction is powerful and he knows she feels it too. Normally he'd be doing all he could to seduce her but there's something about her that makes him hesitate.

After parking his car in a slot reserved for him at the back of the building, he leads her up the stairs to his second-floor apartment. There is a short hallway and stairs leading to the front. The only other apartment on this level is across the hall. She's expecting a typical bachelor's apartment, kind of messy, unorganized, dishes in the sink or maybe an unmade bed. When he unlocks the door, and gestures for her to go in first, she's pleasantly surprised.

It opens to a large common area with a closet and shoe rack on the left, a large kitchen on the right, spotless with copper pots hanging over an island with a wide cooking area and three stools in front of it.

The décor is more modern than she might decorate but the dark masculine colours and chrome work well. White leather couches and a multi-coloured area rug offer a dramatic centerpiece in the living room. Artwork adorns the walls and she recognizes a large rectangular painting over the couch that has to be one of Aurora's, a pastoral scene of lovers in a field of wildflowers, the ardour only hinted at in the position of the nude bodies.

"Is that one of Aurora's paintings? It looks familiar."

"Yes, it is. The paint wasn't even dry when I offered to buy it. I had dropped in to see Max one time and she was in her studio. She let out a whoop that startled both Max and me when we were sharing a beer and she invited us in to see her newest creation. I fell in love with it. The textures, the dreamlike quality of the scene and even though you don't see the faces of the lovers, you can feel their passion. Or maybe it's lust."

He says this watching Jo from out of the corner of his eye. She glances at him when he says lust, and they stare at each other. Unable to stop herself, she steps close and takes his face in her hands to kiss him. The reaction is pure lust. Tongues mingle and hands grope each other. Jo wants him right then but the fact that she hasn't showered for two days, and is feeling grubby, stops her. With her hands on his chest, she steps away.

"I need a shower."

She winks at him.

"A quick one. Where is your bathroom, and can I maybe borrow a robe or a shirt?"

"Of course."

He holds her forearms in his grip and looks at her directly.

"Are you sure, Jo?"

She only nods and offers him another quick peck on the cheek. He goes to a bedroom on the right and returns shortly with a white dress shirt.

"Sorry, I don't have an extra robe, but this should work."

He points to another door across the way.

"The washroom is there. You will find shampoo and soap at the edge of the tub. Towels are in the cabinet on the right. I have a dozen messages that I need to weed out and I have to get my friend to look after the betting for another day or two until we get things sorted out."

She takes the shirt and closes the bathroom door. Stripping quickly,

45

she adjusts the water and steps in, pulling the opaque glass shower door closed. All she can think of is his strong arms and how fast her heart is beating. The scent of his cologne lingers and it makes her think of the beach. She's finished lathering her hair and soaping her body when she hears the click of the striker in the door and the soft whine of unoiled hinges when it fully opens. Looking through the wavy glass, she sees the outline of Bertrand's body and the fleshy tones of his shape. Moistness spreads through her groin and a shiver makes her almost drop the bar of soap.

The glass slides open and Bertrand steps in.

"Can I help you with that?"

She hands him the bar of soap and brushes her hair back with her open fingers. Amorous eyes take in each other's nakedness. Grins of satisfaction cross both their faces. She turns her back to him, her chest in the stream of water.

"Do my back then, please."

They are engulfed in the exploration of each other's bodies, every curve and muscle fondled and caressed with care and amusement. Fingers and lips trace the moisture from sensitive flesh. They can't get out of the shower fast enough. Running wet and naked through the living room, he leads her to his bedroom. The sheets on his wide bed are already pulled down. Passion drives them with a need to satisfy. Jo feeds on the manipulation of experienced hands. Her loneliness and desperate need of love makes her an eager partner. She whispers to him to make it last.

When Jo wakes from a dead sleep, it's to the smell of coffee wafting through the open door of the bedroom. Sitting up on the side of the bed, she puts on the white shirt she finds lying at the foot. She can see Bertrand sitting at the island with a coffee mug in one hand, and a newspaper unfolded in front of him. The other hand holds a pencil. The reading glasses perched on his nose and mussy hair make him look scholarly. But the tattered robe makes him look needy. He notices her movement. Removing his glasses and turning toward her, he offers her a satisfied smile, a happy face.

"I was just about to wake you. It's almost ten and we should eat, and you wanted to grab a change of clothes. Max called saying Brandy was up and alert. She wants to talk to you as soon as she can. You look ravishing by the way."

Jo looks down at her form in the shirt several sizes too large and reaching mid-calf, the sleeves rolled up, the shoulder sagged over her forearm. She can only imagine the state of her hair and red eyes.

"Well thank you kind sir. I like your rugged morning look too, but I'm not sure of that robe."

She starts laughing. He holds up a frayed cuff and turns it this way and that as if inspecting it closely.

"Nothing wrong with this. There are still a few threads holding it together. Besides, it's like an old friend, the last gift my mother gave me. I can't throw it out. I'll just have to wear it out."

He's chuckling when he pours her a cup of coffee. He holds it out to her.

"Black?"

She nods, takes it in both hands and leans against the island, close to him.

"Thanks for last night."

Looking at her directly, his face softens and she can read his eyes.

"Thank *you,* for last night."

There is a moment of quiet, a quick reflection, and neither bother to think where this is going. Jo sets her coffee down and shuffles her feet.

"I need the washroom. I'll be right back."

"There's a new toothbrush on the vanity. Toothpaste in the right drawer."

Jo freshens up and looks around for her clothes. Not seeing them, she tries to remember what she did. Bertrand must've picked them up. Returning to the living room, she finds him dressed in jeans, a white T-shirt under a khaki wool sweater with a V-neck. Solid boots tied to his ankles. Stubble removed from his chin. Hair brushed back off of his forehead.

"Looking good there, partner. Did you see my clothes?"

He nods toward the couch. Jo's clothing, including her panties are folded neatly. She makes a close-lipped smile at him. When she picks them up, the scent of fabric softener tells her they have been washed. Her cheeks colour somewhat at the panties, black with white polka dots, folded in half, and imagines him handling them. She reaches for her clean black jeans, the silk blouse, her socks and her sweater, which was carefully folded off to the side.

"Oh my, Bertrand. How special! You certainly know how to spoil a lady."

A slight bow and a knightly salute.

"You are indeed a lady. And said lady should hustle. I have croissants, cream cheese, apricot jam and brie for breakfast. Lemon tarts for dessert. There are boutiques close by and they'll be open now. And…"

She finishes his statement, knowing what he will say.

"And I need to speak to Brandy."

CHAPTER 8

When Jo and Bertrand leave the apartment, Jo directs him back to the bar where Brandy was abducted. They park the car at the end of the alley and the two of them walk slowly toward the main street, looking for anything they might've missed previously. Jo has a weird feeling about Brandy's disappearance and how they knew she was there that night. Something nags at her but she can't explain the feeling. Realizing it is a long shot but seeing nothing else, they make their way back to discover a man trying to jimmy the lock on the driver's door of the Bertrand's BMW. Bertrand shouts out.

"Hey, what are you doing? Get away from my car."

The man is a bearded, stocky individual. A dark toque is pulled low over his forehead. A hooded jacket is open When alarmed by Bertrand's command, he pulls a gun from an inside pocket and fires at them. They're a good twenty meters from him and the first shot dings off the brown metal dumpster but the second one glazes Bertrand on the upper arm. The bullet misses the muscle by millimeters but singes the surface of his skin. Jo and Bertrand duck behind the garbage bin. Several shots hit the front of it. Jo peeks around the bottom edge to see the shooter with both arms resting on the roof of the vehicle with gun wrapped in a two-hand grip pointed in their direction.

"You okay. Bertrand?"

"Yeah, yeah. The bullet brushed my arm. It stings like crazy but there's no blood that I can see. The bastard owes me a new coat."

Holding the injured arm, Bertrand points to a recessed doorway where they can get out of the shooter's line of sight. Jo nods and bends to pick up a rock the size of a baseball.

"You make a dash for the door and when he's distracted, I'll see if I can hit him. Knock on the door and try to get inside and call for help."

He looks at her with a frown and disbelief.

"You'll hit him with a rock? You can throw that well? I can't leave you here."

"You see anything else to protect ourselves with? Any other ideas? He's being cautious because he doesn't know if we're armed. When he sees you running, he'll step away from the car and I can likely get a good view of him."

"And what if you miss?"

"I don't miss. Get ready."

Jo leans against the edge of the dumpster ready to spring into action. She nods at Bertrand. He takes off like a startled deer and when the man moves aside to aim, Jo steps out from the opposite side and whips the rock like she's Nolan Ryan. The rock hits the man in the face below his left eye and his shot goes into the air. He drops the gun and brings his hands to his face. There is no hesitation from Jo. She runs toward the culprit and attacks him before he can react. From a flying start, she pivots in front of him with her right foot extended and hits him in the solar plexus. He doubles over and Jo takes him out with another kick to the temple. Fifteen seconds.

The man is unconscious, lying crumpled on the ground. Bertrand stands over him, and Jo bends to pick up the gun. Bertrand kneels by the man's head. He removes his hat to better see his face and reveals an upside down cross on his temple.

"*Merde.* How did they find us so soon?"

"There must've been someone else in the house, or a neighbor, that saw your car. They must've sent people to watch out for us."

They're disturbed by a car revving several buildings down the alley screeching in their direction with a gun pointing at them from the driver's window. The man behind the wheel fires at them from the driver's open window. The shots go wild as the car careens toward them. Jo steps in its path and puts a shot through the glass, directly into the centre of the driver's forehead. The car crashes against another dumpster and stalls. The dead man's head rests against the horn, which blares out, the sharp note echoing off the walls.

Bertrand had dropped to the ground when the first shot rang out and looks at Jo with wide-eyed respect. He stands and rushes to her side beside the car where she has pushed the dead man's head off the horn. He remembers her story of being on the run. Bertrand places a hand on her shoulder.

"Good shooting. Now give me the gun and get out of here. I'll call the police now and meet you at Aurora's later. Not sure when but I've got this covered."

He sees Jo's hesitation.

"If you don't want to be found... Jane. Let me get my fingerprints on the gun and go. It was a lucky shot. Go now. I can hear sirens in the background and they're heading this way. Someone likely reported the gunshots."

He can see the gratitude in her eyes when she passes him the gun. He points to the street opposite the end they arrived in last night.

"Go up there and take the first right, go two streets over and head back this way until you come out on the main street that will take you back to Aurora's. You'll recognize things when you get there."

"Thank you, Bertrand. If I'm not at Aurora's when you get clear, they'll know where you can find me."

She turns and runs.

CHAPTER 9

Jo finds Aurora's front door unlocked and knocks before entering to find Max, Aurora and Brandy sitting at the kitchen table. They stare at Jo with anticipation in their eyes. Max meets her in the hallway and notices her harried look.

"Where's Bertrand? Wasn't he supposed to return with you?"

She nods and joins the trio at the table. Brandy rises slowly, holding her side where the largest cut was. She opens her other arm to Jo and embraces her as tight as her wounds will let her. Backing off, her eyes say it all. Aurora rises to get her a cup of fresh coffee.

"Here, drink up. You look like you need it."

"Thank you, Aurora. We had a little surprise when we went out to Bertrand's car earlier."

She explains what took place, to their astonishment.

"... so now the gendarmes are involved. If the biker gang found his place, they'll come looking for Brandy and I know how slow police work is sometimes. We need to relocate each of you temporarily. Is there some place you can all go?"

Max slides an open newspaper toward Jo. It's folded in half, opened at the crime section. On the top of the page in the top right corner is a picture of a teenager's graduation picture of a comely young girl with long straight hair, freckles and dimples surrounding a smile. The story is in French.

"I can't read French. What does this say, and who is she?"

Max and Aurora glance at Brandy who has glassy eyes and is biting her lip so as not to cry.

"She's… she's the girl I met who was feeding me information about the prostitution ring. She's originally from Romania. The picture is two years old. Her body was found yesterday afternoon floating in the Seine, northwest of the city limits. Strangulation. She…"

Brandy breaks down, muttering through a tissue Aurora has given her.

"And… and… it's my fault."

Aurora pulls her chair closer to Brandy and engulfs her in a hug, soothing her with words of assurance that it was not her fault. Jo and Max back her up. Jo is sitting next to her. She puts her hand on top of Brandy's and gives it an affectionate squeeze.

"Brandy, listen to me. You said she came to you. She knew the danger. You tried to help. Now I need you to tell me what happened after they abducted you. Don't leave out any details unless it hurts too much to talk about it. Maybe we can save some other girls."

Brandy straightens up, arms on the table and hands folded. She begins to tell her tale.

"… and when I was doing my interviews at Le Figaro, she bumped into me when I turned onto the sidewalk. I didn't see her coming. I was going to apologize when I noticed she dropped something. I bent to pick up a box of matches and was going to call out when she slipped into the crowd. It was few minutes after noon and there were many people out. I only saw her back for a few seconds. All I could remember was the long legs and short skirt and that it was actually chilly that day."

She pushes her half-filled cup of coffee toward the bottle of cognac. Aurora adds a tot and pushes it back. Her dry mouth clicking, she downs the whole thing. Wiping the dribble from her lip, she carries on.

"I could've sworn I saw her hand wave over her shoulder before she disappeared into the crowd, but I wasn't sure. You know me, nosy and too curious sometimes. The matches were very upscale, wooden matches in an ornate little box. The name and address were embossed gold on a burgundy background. *La Maison Marc Philippe*. Rue de Marseille, in the 3rd Arrondissement. I knew it was near the Canal Saint-Martin. I took the Metro and got off at the Saint-Ambroise station and walked the rest of the way. I was maybe a hundred meters from the restaurant when she stepped out of an alley and scared the dickens out of me. Excuse me but my mouth's dry with all this talking."

She squirms around in her chair and points to the cognac once more. Jo bends forward to look her in the eyes.

"Are you okay Brandy?"

"Yeah, yeah, the cuts are sore and starting to itch. The cognac will help."

Max has been listening intently and grins.

"It'll keep the pain away too, Brandy. Drink up."

She sips the alcohol this time. The smooth liquor glows on the way down.

"I was struck by the young girl's beautiful thick hair. She had only a few minutes. To make matters worse, I couldn't speak French and she used broken English, some words I didn't understand. She said she thought I was a reporter and I didn't contradict her. She told me her name was Talissa and that she and two other girls work out of the lounge in the restaurant. There was some arrangement with the owner but I couldn't understand what she was telling me. In two days from now, she was supposed to meet me at the Eiffel Tower. She was going to run away. There are other women held against their will, some abused, but all are forced into prostitution. She was going to bring me proof before she left."

She sits back with a sigh of resignation, staring into her lap.

"Someone must've seen us. Now she's dead."

Jo touches her lightly on the shoulder.

"Yes, and we need to find out who that is. Do you feel up to telling us about the old house where they kept you? Were the two men the only ones?"

Jo holds up her finger and mimes a writing pad and pen to Aurora who goes to the kitchen and from a drawer removes a small spiral notebook and a pen.

"I want to write some things down. Go ahead Brandy."

"They were two in the car from the club. One drove. The skinny one tied my hands and gagged me with a filthy piece of cloth. I almost threw up on it. I was terrified when they tied me up in the basement. After a long time, maybe half an hour, of being humiliated and fondled, I spit on one of them and he slapped me. He was about to hit me with his fist when two men came down the stairs and one of them yelled at him to back off. I haven't seen that much hate in anybody's eyes before. It was dreadful."

Brandy takes a moment to shake off a bad feeling and tries to understand how such hate could exist from someone she didn't even know.

"I can't forget the look in his eyes, but I didn't have time to dwell on it. The two men that arrived were so different, like night and day. One was a biker for sure. Rough weathered face with a bushy beard. Tattoos on his hands and the upside down cross on his neck. Wore his biker colours over his jacket. Much bigger than his accomplice. He had an odd look in his eyes, like he didn't care for the other guy much. The other man was well dressed in a white shirt and red tie under a black suit. His grey overcoat looked expensive, like soft wool. He had a thin face, slicked back hair and a scar on his jawbone. He never touched me but he gave the commands. They kept drilling me to find out what Talissa told me. I thought that if I said anything, her life would be in danger. So I didn't, even when they cut me and hit me. They swore they would kill me if I didn't tell the truth. It went on for over an hour. Finally, the slicked-up guy said to leave me and he'd be back in the morning and it would be my last chance to tell him the truth."

Brandy pauses, a clouded look in her eyes.

"And holding out didn't save her."

Brandy can't contain herself any longer and the tears flow, a release of pent-up fear. Aurora holds her and rocks back and forth, soothing her as she might a child. Jo and Max watch, she with a building anger, Max with sorrow. Jo speaks softly to Brandy.

"One more question, Brandy, and then you can rest. Did you hear any of the names of the two men that came later?"

Brandy is nodding. Aurora has given her a tissue to wipe her eyes.

"The dressed-up man was called Albert. They spoke French but I recognized the name."

"Any names of the other girls who work from the lounge?"

Brandy shakes her head.

"Ok. Go lie down Brandy. Get some rest."

"What are you going to do, Jo?"

"As soon as Bertrand returns, we're going to the restaurant and find one of the other girls."

Max reminds her that whoever was watching will be on the lookout and it might not be a good idea for Jo to approach them, especially when she doesn't speak French. She tells them not to worry.

"Bertrand is going to hire a prostitute."

CHAPTER 10

Bertrand spent twenty minutes having his wound dressed, told that it was superficial and to watch for infection. Then he spent two hours in the presence of the police until his friend Emile came upon the site and vouched for Bertrand. The investigating officer was not too keen on having a dead biker on his hands but it was chalked up to self-defense. On the other hand, he had a keen interest in the injured one, a Belgian crook with warrants out for his arrest in his country.

At present, he and Jo are two blocks from a restaurant, watching the coming and goings of the patrons. They sit in a café by the window, nursing their coffees and desserts. They have to dawdle and have their coffees refilled twice before they see two young women approaching the premises. They are unsure of who is who but the short skirts and heavily made-up faces distinguish them from the regular patrons. Neither one has eyes that look happy. Jo notices them first and nods towards the women, making eye contact with Bertrand, who has his back to them.

"Those ladies look promising, Bertrand. Go now and ask if they know Talissa."

"And if they don't?"

"Link up with one anyway and separate them. Make sure you still have the key to the room at the hotel we booked."

He withdraws a card, much like a credit card, which will gain him entry to room 202 at the *Auberge Trésor Caché*. Jo removes a similar one from her jacket pocket.

"Meet you there."

Jo zips up her jacket. Because it's warmer than yesterday, although overcast, she tucks her toque in her side pocket but replaces her gloves. Bertrand waits a couple of minutes after she leaves before approaching the two women who are lingering off to the side smoking their cigarettes. He removes a cigarette from his own package. When he is near them, they stop chatting and watch him. Both offer fake alluring smiles. Bertrand pokes the unlit cigarette in his mouth and decides to talk to the one who looks to be the youngest of the duo. Her dyed blonde hair seems much too bright to be natural.

"Do you have a light?"

She eyes her partner who nods, then reaches into a small clutch strung over her shoulder. Removing a slim brass lighter, she flicks the flame open and holds it up to Bertrand's cigarette. She looks at him directly.

"Is a light all you need, Monsieur?"

"I was actually looking for some company for an hour or two. I'm looking for Talissa."

The women steal a quick glance at each other, then both shake their heads. Bertrand catches the hint of recognition of the name but he doesn't pursue any further inquiry regarding Talissa. He knows they know who he's talking about. He needs to get one alone. He just shrugs as if it doesn't matter. Seeing Bertrand as a potential customer, the blonde sidles closer to him so she can whisper in his ear. He can feel her breasts against his chest. Normally this would be enough to arouse him but he actually feels pity for these women if what Jo has told him is true. Her French is clipped, the language not her everyday tongue.

"Two hours would require a gift."

He raises his brow as if he doesn't understand.

"How large would this gift have to be? And how do I know you're not a gendarme in disguise?"

The women share a laugh over his last question. The blonde leans toward him, opens her jacket and shifting the neckline of her blouse shows him one of her breasts, the nipple taut and rosy.

"A gendarme would not do that now, would she? That would be entrapment. For two hours, the gift would have to be two hundred euros."

Bertrand plays his part well and appears to think it over, not wanting to appear too willing at the large amount of money.

"That seems expensive for just two hours of your time."

As she moves closer to him again, he can smell her cologne, something spicy, which makes him think of cinnamon. She stares at him and licks her lips in a seductive manner. The smile is practiced.

"I'm worth much more."

He plays the game and nods. Offering her his arm, he points his chin up the street.

"Let's go, then."

"You have a place?"

He waves the hotel key in front of her.

"Not far from here. Shall we?"

She nods at the other lady and takes Bertrand's arm. They set off toward the hotel and her partner enters the lounge. The blonde is relieved. Most of her johns are older or overweight or both. This one is extremely good looking and she wonders why he would hire a prostitute. She's always nervous but she doesn't see any malice in his eyes. They don't speak until they enter the lobby. He releases her arm and has her proceed up the stairs before him.

"What do I call you?"

"You can call me Tanya."

"That's a nice name. Over there. Room 202."

He slides the card in the offered slot, which responds with the blinking of a green light. The lock clicks. He pushes the door open and waves her in. They enter a short hallway with a closed washroom door on the right. Removing her jacket, she drops it along with her clutch on a padded chair by the desk with the TV on it. She turns to Bertrand who is standing there watching her.

"I need the gift up front, please. And what do I call you?"

Before he can reply, Jo steps out of the washroom and faces them both. She smiles at the young girl.

"You can call me Jane and this here," she points to Bertrand, "is Joseph."

Tanya backs off a bit with a surprised look on her face. Her English is better than her French.

"You didn't say anything about a threesome, Joseph. We may have to renegotiate my gift."

Bertrand leans back against the desk and rests his butt against it, crosses his arms and lets Jo take over. He looks at his partner.

"Her name is Tanya."

"Ok, Tanya. There's not going to be a threesome or a twosome or anything. Whatever you and Joseph agreed on is what you get. We promise. We just want to talk."

The prostitute has a worried look on her face. Her dark green eyes go wide and she steps away from them, closer to the window.

"What... what do you want to talk about?"

"Talissa is dead."

The young girl hangs her head and holds her face in both hands. Her body begins to shake and her knees wobble. The moaning precedes soft sobs and her tears spill over. Jo reaches to comfort her and guides her to sit on the bed. Bertrand retrieves several tissues from the bathroom and hands them to her. They let her cry for a moment.

"She never returned on Sunday. We feared the worst but were told she was working another part of the city and staying with other women. That's what they say when someone disappears."

The poor girl is shaking. Jo sits beside her and takes one of her hands in her own. She tells Tanya what little they know.

"You're from Romania too?"

She nods. The girl's memories of her homeland cause a weak smile.

"Yes, a small village called Scapau."

"How did you end up here?"

"There were ads online of families in Paris looking for an *au pair* and I wanted to travel. I applied and was accepted. But when I arrived, I was held outside the city at a farmhouse where other girls were kept and locked in rooms. When I refused to cooperate, the rough men slapped me many times until a man in a suit showed me a picture of my younger brother and my parents. He told me if I went to the police or didn't do what he told me, all three of them would die a terrible death. That was almost a year ago."

It's too much for her and she starts crying again. Jo reassures her they are there to help.

"How? How can you possibly help? Are you going to Romania to protect my family?"

"I expect the threat is enough to keep you in line. I doubt there is anyone standing over your family. If they had to come good on their threat, they'd have to send someone. We won't let that happen, will we B... Joseph?"

"*Non.* You are safe with us. We need some information. When the two hours are up, you can go back with the money we will give you. You'll have to trust us."

59

She wipes away the tears and nods.

"What do you want to know?"

"Who runs the show, and where do they keep you?"

Tanya explains the set up. There are seven other girls being held captive and manipulated with the same threats as her - a promise to kill their family or a loved one. Their passports were taken from them and they were all given fake IDs. Talissa was going to take a chance and had planned on running away. She figured she would get back to Romania somehow and warn her family.

The women are being held at a farmhouse twenty kilometers out of the city, in the northern reaches of the commune of Bouqueval, and brought in six days a week from midafternoon until late in the night, or in most cases early in the morning. There is a house with several apartments not far from here where they can go to freshen up between johns. She gives them the address. As far as she knows, there is no one living on the upper floors. There are always three men here in the city. And always two, sometimes more, at the farmhouse. They are all part of a motorcycle gang. She doesn't know where their club is or where they keep their bikes. Jo takes out a small notepad and a pen. Tanya draws them a rough map. Jo takes it and not knowing the city, passes it to Bertrand.

"Why three in the city, Tanya?"

"To protect the girls, the house. Le Croix runs this part of the arrondissement but the Algerians have been sending some of their women and there is some... how you say... turf wars."

"Do you know where the farmhouse is, Joseph?"

"Roughly but I don't think we will have trouble finding it."

Jo turns her attention back to Tanya.

"And two or three at the house in the country. How and when do they round all you girls up at night?"

"Usually around three in the morning. There's a lounge on *Rue Chrysanthème*, owned by the *Lagrange* family. We meet there and two of the men drive us back in a van."

Jo perks up at the mention of two.

"So, when they come to the city to pick you up, there might only be one or two back at the farmhouse?"

Tanya nods right away.

"At roughly four thirty in the morning, you are all at the same house together?"

Tanya nods.

"Usually."

Jo's mind is already working. Whatever they do will have to be done at night when everyone least expects it.

"Tell me about the man in the suit."

It sounds like the same man that held Brandy in the basement. Jo then asks her about the bigger man, the biker.

"He's the worst. Forces himself on us. The other bikers are not allowed to touch us but he can whenever he wants. He's a pig. I think he is the boss. The call him *Le Tigre*. He's mean, very mean. He always arrives with the man in the suit."

Jo asks her a couple more questions about the safe house. She wonders how can she take advantage of it and what damage could she do to the bikers. Send them a message maybe. Disorient them. Passing her note pad to Talissa, she prompts her to write.

"Mark down the women's names and what village or city they are from if you know. I'll do what I can to protect their families. I know some people that know some people... you understand?"

Jo digs out a bunch of euros and looks at Bertrand. "Two hundred."

She counts it out and passes it to Tanya. She checks her watch.

"Stay here for another hour, Tanya. There's a clock by the bed. Don't go back on the street until three o'clock. Give us a little time to protect your families and we'll come for you. Joseph and I are going to be busy, slow these guys down, shake them up a bit. Don't say a word Tanya. Your life... and ours depend on it. You understand?"

Tanya embraces her. She decides to trust this stranger. There's something in her eyes that tells her to.

"Yes, yes I do. Thank you, Jane... and Joseph."

Head down, Tanya goes to the washroom to redo her makeup. Bertrand and Jo leave the hotel keys on the bed and exit the building. When they are on the sidewalk, Jo stops and steps back to let people by and whispers to Bertrand.

"Do you have a gun?"

"Oh, oh. What do we need a gun for?"

Looking around, she waves him to talk lower but no one is listening.

"We can raid their safe house, put it out of commission."

"What good would that do?"

"Right now I'm so pissed off at those ruffians, those animals. I want to put a dent in their operation."

Bertrand takes her shoulders in his hands and looks at her directly. He adores how feisty she is.

"Maybe you should take a deep breath, calm down."

She shakes him off.

"I am calmed down. I'm going with or without you, Bertrand."

Bertrand is not a guy to back down from danger. He is no gunman. But he saw the bruises on the dead girl's neck and the helplessness in her eyes. He's not a coward either.

"Ok, ok, ok…. what am I getting into?"

"I asked if you had a gun."

"No, but I know where we can get one, probably two.

CHAPTER 11

Fully automatic weapons are illegal to own by private citizens in Paris. If one purchases or possesses one illegally, they can be punishable up to seven years in prison. Semi-automatics are different but you can get in trouble without permits. It's a chance Jo and Bertrand are willing to take. A cab ride takes them into the red-light district, near the 9th Arrondissement. Bertrand directs the cabbie to a narrow street that is dark and dreary even in the middle of the afternoon. He tells him to stop next to a series of rundown apartment building and asks Jo how much money she has. She tells him, and he asks for another one hundred euros. Then he tells her to wait in the taxi for him. The cabbie asks him to be quick. He's not comfortable in this part of the city. Bertrand is back in less than ten minutes with a paper bag clutched under one elbow. Jumping in the cab he tells the driver to return to where he picked them up.

When they get out of the cab, Bertrand pulls Jo into the nearest alley. They are only two minutes from the safe house Tanya told them about. Opening the bag, he removes a Glock 17 and passes it to Jo. She loves the Glock. It's light and dependable. She releases and pulls back the slide and looks through the barrel. There is an extra magazine in the bag with 17, 9mm Parabellum bullets. Bertrand takes the Berretta Nano. It's a smaller gun, good for back up with six bullets in the magazine and one in the chamber. There are two single stack clips with it. Same 9mm ammo. A full box comes with the guns.

Jo is impressed.

"Don't ask."

"Ok. You know how to use that?"

"Not really but you just pull the trigger, right?"

"There's a little more to it than that."

She shows him how to hold it, how to insert and remove the magazine and how to aim using a two-handed grip

"If you don't have time to aim properly and we probably won't, shoot for the largest part of the body. The torso. Don't try anything fancy. If we need to use these, you'd better be ready. Now hide it and let's go case the house."

The building is similar to all the crowded edifices on the older streets of Paris. Crowded together like books on a shelf, they are deep and narrow, mostly three or four levels with all brick or stone fronts. The one Tanya pointed out is more rundown than its neighbours' and could use some fixing, Jo expects it remains as it is so as not to draw attention. The first levels feature retail establishments, bars and an old disco for the eighties crowd. A few have colourful awnings but most have faded over time. The street is cobbled with enough pedestrian traffic to cover the comings and goings of the call girls.

A burly man, big of gut, is leaning with his back to the building, one foot propped up on the brick as if ready to push himself off. He's wearing a heavy jacket with a hood, unzipped this afternoon due to the warmer weather. His bushy hair and week's stubble on his fat chin makes him look like he's in a bad mood. He's wearing gloves with the fingertips cut off and blue bib coveralls. His biker buddies consider him a sharp dresser. He's glancing everywhere.

Jo and Bertrand see him when they approach. They're on the opposite side of the street coming towards his left. He's four feet from the main door. He's looking their way as he eyeballs the group of teenage girls. So Jo and Bertrand duck behind a loading truck parked halfway up the sidewalk. A pimply-faced young man is delivering bagged snacks to one of the bodegas and pays no attention to them. Jo peers around the edge of the truck and sizes up the doorman. Maybe five feet nine or ten, two hundred pounds. Broad chest and no neck, looks strong. If she has to, the gut and the groin will be the weak spots. Maybe a little gun persuasion will be enough. When the young man returns with his trolley for more confections she backs away and talks low to Bertrand.

"I'm going to go ahead on this side until I'm past him and can cross over to approach him from the other direction. When you see me, run across and distract him, draw his attention away. You'll have to do the talking if he doesn't understand English."

"Got it. Then what?"

"Then we're going inside and see what we can do to mess things up for them. Send them a message. You up to this?"

"No, I'm scared shitless."

She laughs easy, and it feels good. She rolls her shoulders and loosens up. Passersby look at her oddly.

"Me too, handsome. Now let's go."

Jo steps in tune, just a half step behind, with two gabbing and laughing ladies so that it looks as if they could be together. It doesn't matter. Big Boy at the door never even glances at her and she's a good distance past him when she waits for three autos to go by, and then scoots across. With her hand in one pocket holding the gun, she keeps her head down, her baseball hat low on her brow. When she's fifty feet from the man, she sees Bertrand run across the street. He's waving a cigarette in his hand. The man has a cigarette of his own, half burnt and he offers it as a lighter to Bertrand. While he's watching Bertrand, leery of the man's presence, Jo walks up behind him and jams her gun in his side. With practiced French, she uses her serious cop voice.

"Ne bouge pas. J'ai une arme."

Bertrand smiles at his surprised look. A little fear flashes in the man's eyes for a second but quickly turns to anger. He knows enough to stay still. Bertrand puffs on his cigarette and flicks the man's butt on the street. He steps close to him with an animated face as if they've been friends for a long time. He speaks to him in French through a phony smile.

"Who's inside?"

The biker eyes him up and down, not seeming impressed. The man grins, his wide face exposing a few lower missing teeth.

"More than you and your girlfriend can handle, pretty boy."

Jo doesn't understand what he said but she understands the way it was delivered. She rams the blunt edge of the gun into his ribs. Her poke is hard enough to penetrate the coat and she jams the fat against a rib. He drops the grin and grunts. Bertrand cocks his brows.

"You were saying?"

"Two more."

"Where are they now? "

"I don't know. Anywhere in there. They hang out in the kitchen a lot, drink coffee all day. I don't know."

Bertrand tells her what he said, never taking his eyes off the man. Jo pushes harder with the gun, leaning right into the guy. He can feel her breath on his cheek. She's taller than him. She notices that he is paying attention when they speak.

"You understand English?"

A quick nod.

"Is there a back door?"

Another nod.

"Is the front door locked?"

A quick shake. She pushes on him to go toward the front door. He balks and stays still.

"What do you want?"

Bertrand stands closer, as if confiding in a friend.

"We have a message from the Algerians."

Jo likes that and jabs the man with the gun.

"You first. Enter very slowly like you're in no hurry. Bertrand stay close behind me and cover me."

The man starts to move up the three steps to the wide door and she walks in tandem, same step, same timing. He stops at the top.

"You'll be sorry, lady."

"Not as sorry as you. Now get your fat ass moving."

What he didn't tell them is that his two accomplices are always in the living room, probably playing cards. Their guns are always within reach. Doing as he's told, he unlatches the door and hesitates before opening it all the way, looking back at Jo and Bertrand.

"You sure you want to do this?"

"Stop stalling."

The hesitation is a signal and when Jo enters closely behind, somebody to her right sticks the barrel of a gun in her ear.

CHAPTER 12

Big Boy's accomplice shows his inexperience. He should've waited until everyone cleared the door. When he threatened Jo, in his haste, he didn't realize someone was close behind. Bertrand sees the gun and, as inexperienced as he is, he raises his gun and shoots at the man's hand. He's so close he can't miss. The shot goes through the back of the hand. The bullet misses the handle of the gun by millimeters and sails on through at 820 miles an hour. The gun clatters to the floor and like the gunshot, the man's scream can be heard all over the street. People nearby run in all directions amid the chaos. At least four of them dial 17, the emergency number for the police in France.

The third accomplice has the misfortune of standing in line of the bullet thinking he had the front door covered by standing directly in front of it seven feet back. The same bullet takes him in the right lung, a whisper above the heart. The sucking chest wound won't kill him right away, but he'll have a hard time breathing until he succumbs to death by exsanguination.

Jo recoils from the gun shot so close to her that she goes deaf in her right ear and cringes from the pain. She falls toward an empty space in the entryway, tucking in tight to take it on her shoulder. Using the momentum of her roll, she lands on her back. The big man she was using as a shield, sees his chance and lunges forward with a raised steel-toed boot. Jo has little room to maneuver. She falls at the bottom of a stairway. Curling into a ball and with her back braced, she kicks out at the space between the upraised boot and the other leg. Crushed nuts, anyone?

His eyes bug out. His ugly face is slobbering when the pain hits. His head goes down. Jo recoils like a rubber band and strikes again, connecting with his jaw. The blow knocks him backward against the wall with a hard whack to the head. He passes out from the impact and topples forward, landing on his face.

A gun hot startles Jo and she scrambles to her feet, rubbing her ear. Bertrand is standing a good step into the house with his two hands around a smoking gun. The man with the hole in his hand is on the floor under the archway with another hole in his chest, an inch lower than his partner. He dies right away. An eight-inch dagger is still clutched angrily in his other fist. His face is serene and unblemished. Too young, thinks Jo as she shakes Bertrand out of his stupor.

"Get it together. It was them, or us. Listen."

A siren is low on the horizon, announcing its imminent arrival. Jo pulls at Bertrand's jacket and heads toward a hallway leading to a kitchen in the back.

"Put your gun away. Follow me."

Finding the rear exit is easy. It's right off the kitchen. However they are slowed down as she has to fiddle with a faulty lock. There is more than one siren now and they're getting louder. Finding the right twist, she finally gets the door open and starts running with Bertrand close behind. They're in an alley. Bertrand points to a street ten houses away, opposite the street they were on before, where it's busy and normal. She nods and pushes him forward. She wants to bring up the rear.

"Get us to the nearest metro station."

CHAPTER 13

The metro is calm before the onslaught of workers going home. There are many empty seats with only ten other commuters spread around the car. Jo is next to Bertrand, both sitting forward with their elbows on their knees. His bangs are hanging down his forehead, Jo's hat pushed back from her brow. Both of them are adjusting to the after-effects of their running and the euphoria of danger. Eventually, their breathing becomes steady. A slight ringing remains but Jo's hearing is returning to normal. She turns her head to look at him.

"You okay?"

"I'm not sure. I've never killed a man before."

Jo knows the feeling. In her rookie year as a cop, she shot a woman. Line of duty, saved one of her buddies, got a citation, pats on the back, but the woman's dying face still nags at her.

"Yeah, it's rough. But you did good. He could've done some dam-age with that knife. It was a good shot. I should be pissed at you shoot-ing so close to my head. I'm still having trouble hearing out of that ear."

She tries to lighten the mood with a pat on his knee and a tight smile.

"Tell me when we are close to the Seine. We can dump your gun."

"Why mine?"

"Ballistics can match up a slug they might find to that weapon. Bet-ter to be safe. No trails, no evidence if we get caught with these."

"People will have seen us."

"Only our backs, mainly yours. With all due respect, there's nothing different about you to stand out. There will be a bunch of witnesses and they'll tell different stories because they will think they saw us. A lot of people like to help the police. We'll get rid of the gun to be safer. I expect, from what Tanya told us, and your quick thinking, they'll blame the Algerians."

"Ok. We're coming up to the *Gare d'Austerlitz*. It's an elevated station and near the Seine. We can find a spot there."

The train stops amid the shrieking of brakes and people waiting at the doors to get out. Jo and Bertrand blend into the crowd and head out on the street. It's a short walk to the river through a copse of hardwoods and a large wharf where several barges are double-parked. They follow the street until they are under the *Pont d'Austerlitz*. When the road is clear and there's no one around, Bertrand heaves the gun eight meters out into the water.

They're not far from the Sorbonne and start walking in that direction, hoping to find a café. Jo hasn't eaten since the morning and her stomach is churning. The sky is turning pink with the sun settling over the western skyline. The streets are in shadow and busy with people hustling for home or other destinations. There is a small pub near the university and when they enter, there are only a few seats vacant. Finding a small table near the rear, they join the crowd. The smell of onions on the grill competes with the scent of beer on tap and the aroma of fresh coffee. A murmur of conversation in multiple languages buzzes in the air. Jo has to sit close to Bertrand to hear him properly.

"What do you want to do next, Jo?"

"We need to get back to your place and then you can drive me back to the inn. I need to change and decide our next step. I hope this isn't hurting your business."

"Don't worry about that. My buddy, Armand and I switch over occasionally when we need a break. And, yes, I can take you to your room. I think someone mentioned you're staying where Max hangs his hat."

"Yes."

They're interrupted by the young waitress with rings in her ears and one through her nose. Dark-framed glasses make her blue eyes bigger. She has a cheerful lilt to her voice and flirts with her eyes at Jo's handsome partner. They each order beers and the special, Bavarian sausage and sauerkraut with mashed potatoes. After she leaves, Jo leans in closer.

70

"Do you think you can find the farmhouse?"

He pulls the squashed napkin from his jacket pocket and straightens it out in front of them.

"Yes, I'm familiar with Bouqueval. It's northwest of the inn you are staying at."

She looks at him with desire in her eyes and a warm smile.

"Maybe you should stay the night and we can have a look in the morning then decide what we will do."

"Maybe so. I'd like that."

He returns her smile and then a frown crosses his face.

"Why are you doing this Jo? I mean, I know you were a cop before, but aren't you here on holidays. Or supposed to be?"

"I don't know sometimes, Bertrand. I had hoped to spend time alone and sort through the things that nag at me. But my conscience won't let me. I hate when bad people take advantage of others, disrupt lives in their greed for money. I can't ignore human suffering. I was trained to uphold the law. It's been drilled into me. A few times over the last two days, I thought about getting on a plane and going, but I can't."

They each think about what she said for a few moments until Melanie, their waitress, brings them steaming plates of nourishment. They eat their meal mainly in silence, Jo thinking of what she's going to do after she helps the young girls. Trouble seems to follow her everywhere. She probably won't be able to stick around Paris after this. She knows well enough they can't take down the Lagrange family. But maybe she and Bertrand can put a dent in their business.

Bertrand is surprised by his feelings for Jo. He finds her fascinating though perhaps a little lost at the moment. Tall and slight of frame, she doesn't look dangerous. But he's seen her in action. He trusts her instincts and won't let her down. He just hopes he survives this escapade.

When they finish their meal and refuse the offer for dessert, Jo picks up the bill and leaves a hefty tip for Melanie. When they are outside, she takes one arm and smiles at her friend.

"Let's go get your car, Bertrand, and you can make me forget all about this nonsense for the night."

CHAPTER 14

It's a few minutes after eleven the next morning when Jo and Bertrand get on Highway A1 going north. Jo is still basking in the glow of their lovemaking. She was able to put aside her troubles when wrapped in Bertrand's strong arms. He's an exceptional lover, teasing, prolonging their release. She could fall in love with this man but she won't let herself have that luxury, as she is uncertain of her future in Paris after tonight when they raid the farm – that is if all goes as planned. She smiles inwardly because right now there isn't much of a plan other than freeing the women.

They intend to find the house and pretend they're looking for directions, or some such fantasy, to get them close. Bertrand gets off the highway and heads east toward the upper reaches of the Commune of Bouqueval, where there are a few farms still in operation. He has to pull over to study the rough map Tanya drew on the napkin. Cruising back and forth, they look for Chemin Benoit. There are no signs in the vicinity with the name on it. But Jo notices the end of a square post beside a dirt road that leads up a sharp incline through a small, forested area.

"Stop Bertrand. There is a post sticking up at the edge of the ditch beside the last road. It might tell us which road it is. Back up and I'll have a look."

She gets out of the car and lifts the post up. It's been broken off at ground level. It is a green metallic sign and the name *Chemin Benoit* is clearly displayed when she pulls it up. She drops it back on the ground and gets back in the car.

"This is the road. Drive up slowly. Tanya said it's the last farm and it has an old concrete silo which is falling apart."

Bertrand backs up enough to turn up the lane and follows the dirt road. At the top of the rise and through a shallow strip of trees, there are open fields on the right, crusted along the perimeters with ice. More trees edge the left. Bristles of reaped grains stick up through the light covering of snow like a brush cut.

The first farm they encounter has long been abandoned. The house has plywood over the windows and doorway. Although there are tracks in the driveway, there are no footprints. Two hundred meters ahead, in a slight dip in the land, the second one is inhabited and in better condition. It's surrounded by century old oaks, forming a perimeter of privacy. Farm machinery sits idle helter-skelter on the property. Beside a two-storey wooden barn with white doors are several beef cattle gathered around a trough filled with hay. Their breath floats in the air like small clouds. No silo. They drive another three hundred meters before they see another farmhouse and a dead end. There is more activity here. Two men are working over a car in the yard with the hood up. Two other vehicles are parked beside it. One of them is a passenger van. A concrete silo is beside the dilapidated barn but the house is in good shape with smoke spiraling out the chimney. The men notice Jo and Bertrand approaching and turn toward them. Jo notices the shorter one's hand go to a pocket and stay there.

"Stop about twenty feet away from them…"

She notices his confused look.

"About five meters, sorry. I forget you're not familiar with the Imperial distances. Can you please get out and ask them where…, I don't know…, make up a name and ask them where his farm is? Make it look like we're lost."

Bertrand does so and notices the men moving toward their vehicle with heavy scowls on their faces. One of them has an upside down cross tattooed on his neck. Definitely bikers. The shorter one is making it obvious he's holding a gun in his pocket. Jo watches Bertrand talking to them and pointing at the house. The two men are shaking their heads. Jo scans the property, the naked hedgerow, the fields, the woods across the road, three vehicles, one of which is a large van for maybe twelve passengers. Besides that there is another smaller building, the barn and the ruined silo. No women are evident. Looking behind her, she can only see the roof and tall trees of the last farmhouse. Very private. Before Bertrand returns to the car, she's seen all she needs and notices the tallest of the bikers laughing. They are all looking at her. She puts on her best smile and waves. The two strangers wave back and return to the car they were working on. Bertrand gets back in the car and backs up onto the road to turn around.

"What did you tell them, and why were you all laughing?"

"I told them we were looking for the Renault farm, Marthe and Arsene Renault. They of course never heard of it, and there is no one in this area that they know of with that name. The shorter one was looking aggressive and I was nervous so I made a joke. I told them you were reading the map and it was your fault we were lost. Typical woman. Hope you don't mind."

She waves him off.

"Truth is, I'm not the best at reading maps. I'm so dependent on my GPS, so you weren't lying."

"Did you see everything you needed to?"

"Yes, and I already have a plan."

"*Bon*. Where to next?"

"Bank, clothing store, men's preferably, and a hardware store. I need boots, too. Then your arms dealer, one more stop and back to your place."

Bertrand slows the car before turning on the highway and looks at Jo and the way her brow is furled in concentration. He imagines the wheels turning in her head.

"I get a weird sensation when you mentioned one other stop. I think I'm about to be taken advantage of?"

"We need to talk to Tanya. Make sure of our timing. Find out how many men and any precautions they've taken since our escapade yesterday. And… I want to know she's ok."

"So, I have to hire a prostitute?"

"Know any other way?"

"What if there are people watching? Someone who may have seen me on Wednesday? We don't want to get her in trouble.

CHAPTER 15

When they return to Bertrand's apartment, it's late in the evening. The sky is clear and the moon's getting fat. They could only connect with a dealer for Jo's more unique request, other than another handgun, at ten o'clock in the 2nd District. They take two trips each to unload the SUV, bringing in shopping bags, all new except one which is scuffed up and wrinkled from usage, something wrapped in a blanket, and a pizza.

Dumping everything onto the couch, they set up the pizza in the nook off the kitchen with a round Formica and chrome table from the sixties and four matching chairs. Manly clutter is scattered around the kitchen in the form of a cordless drill parked by the toaster and an empty beer bottle in front of the antique bread box. Bertrand lights a scented candle, takes out plates, utensils and napkins. While he opens a bottle of wine, he watches from the corner of his eye as Jo relaxes in one of the chairs and unfolds her coat from her shoulders to rest it on the back of the chair. She takes off her hat and shakes out her short curls. From her scrunched brow, he can tell she's deep in thought. Her profile, the strong chin and slender nose, makes him melts when he looks at her.

"What are you thinking about?"

"I think you should stay out of this. I'm having second thoughts of you volunteering, Bertrand. This is dangerous. You could be killed."

"So could you."

"Yes, I know but I'm trained for this. I've been confronting the enemy all my adult life. It's silly to say but it's in my blood. I get a rush

75

when I put these people away. You remember what you said when you killed that man back in the city. It happens. You deal with it. You never get comfortable with it but acting in self-defense has no shame."

"I'm okay now when I think of the knife he was waving at me."

He pours the wine and gives her a glass.

"Let's eat up. I'm starving. Then we can get organized."

He digs out the pizza cutter and swipes it through the dough three times. He slips two slices each on the plates and joins her at the table. The aroma of rosemary in the sauce and the stringy cheese makes her stomach gurgle. He looks up after his first bite to see her chewing slowly with closed eyes and he can tell she likes it. They don't talk about what will happen later as they dine and empty the wine bottle. Jo tells him about when she was growing up, but nothing of her father's crimes. He shares a few anecdotes from his childhood in Villeneuve-Loubet, near Nice. How he ended up in Paris. His bookie business. So easy now with everything online. By the end of the meal, he shocks Jo with a loud burp.

"*Excuse.* It's good. Don't you think?"

She giggles at him and points at her empty plate.

"I do."

Finishing the last of her wine, she sits back feeling relaxed for the first time since the night at the club.

"Do you still have family in Villeneuve-Loubet?"

"Only an aunt, she's...," he rubs his chin, "... you would call her an old maid in English, I think. *Une veille fille.* My father's sister, she lives in the home they grew up in. And I have a sister that lives in Ethiopia. She runs a medical clinic with her partner. Both are doctors and humanitarians."

His voice has the softness of memory, sweet on the tongue.

"I still own my father's house. On the Rivière Loup. Two and a half kilometers from the Mediterranean. I usually rent it out. I occupy it every September for the whole month when my tenants go sailing. The couple who were staying there moved to Belgium last summer and I haven't rented it since."

He describes the hills and mountains in the distance, the expanse of the sea, the aroma of its bounty, the gentle flow of the river behind his house in the fall, how it changes to a rushing stream in the spring and the flowerbeds his mother so tenderly nourished. Jo basks in the fond images that spring forth through his words.

"I wish I could show it to you."

"You make it sound so dreamy, Bertrand. Maybe we can when this is over. I'll have to get out of Paris. I can't be around you people; somebody is bound to be looking for me... us. You know that, right? When you volunteered. You won't be able to stick around Paris, at least for a while. They already know where you live."

"Yes. I've been thinking of that. Perhaps, it would be good to leave the city for a few weeks or months. I can do my business from anywhere just as well. We could go."

It's more of a question rather than a statement. Jo doesn't want to fall for this man. She studies him as he cleans up the table. His sweater is tight across his broad shoulders, his hair a little long. She loves his buns. It could be fun. But she promises herself - no commitments.

"Let's do it."

She rises and he takes her in his arms. Their kisses are teasing. She has to shrug out of his grip and ignore the desire she feels.

"Not now, my friend. We need to check our gear before getting some rest."

She looks around for a garbage bin with the folded pizza box in her hand until he takes it from her.

"I got it. I'll finish up here. Go check the hardware."

The first is her pack with a change of clothes, cosmetics bag and her Glock. She sets it on the floor. The next is a plain brown shopping bag with twine handles and a moustache logo, the words *L'Maison Noel* on the front. It contains black cargoes, black T-shirts, black socks and black fleeces. She separates them by size. The next is from a hardware store. Two rolls of duct tape. Two palm sized Maglites. Batteries. A twenty-four-inch length of a one-and-a-half-inch diameter hardwood dowel which the man at the store conveniently cut for her, a twelve-inch piece of nylon rope, black gloves and black toques. The third bag has her new boots.

The fourth bag is the crumpled one. Inside are four flashbangs, less-lethal grenades designed to have a loud bang and intense flash of light to disorient the enemy. She probably won't need four but she's bringing them all anyway. Two smoke grenades. In an oily rag is another Glock 17, a bit more scratched up than Jo's but it looks solid. She places it on one of the empty bags so no gun oil gets on the couch. Unwrapping the blanket, she removes the two bullet proof vests. Tactical vests. Several useful pockets over Kevlar. Black. Sets them on the last empty space on the couch.

Standing back to look at everything with her hands on her hip, she listens to the low strains of the first movement of Vivaldi's Four Seasons in the background. Bertrand stands beside her.

"We have quite a collection. Have you used one of those flash things before?"

"Yeah. They're used by police and the military. Good for causing panic. But they can be lethal if they explode close to a person."

"What do we need to do to get ready?"

"Go get a rag and start cleaning the gun. Wipe it all down good. I'll check it later. I'm going to load each vest with two flashbangs and a smoke grenade."

While he's sitting in an easy chair next to the couch cleaning the gun, she shows him the triggering device on the grenades.

"The smoke grenades have a pin. And a handle. Pull the pin and throw. The handle will spring open on its own. Don't let go of the handle until you throw it. The flashbangs are the same. Think of a real grenade. Same principle. You have one point five seconds after releasing the handle. These are good ones. Explosions on each end so it won't become a projectile."

"How will I know when to use them if we get separated?"

"We'll get separated for sure."

She smiles at his look of surprise. He's rubbing his goatee, a worried air in his eyes. Jo reaches for a smaller bag, red plastic with a black logo of a lightning bolt. She removes two battery packs and headsets with Bluetooth so they can communicate with each other. They're bigger than she's familiar with but they'll have their toques and the night.

"We have these, remember?"

"Right. What's the range?"

"A hundred feet, about thirty meters."

He passes her the gun.

"Gun's clean."

She clicks on the mag release. Holds the slide in an awkward grip and using her other hand, clicks the slide lock. The slide snicks forward. She removes it and takes out the spring, then the barrel. After inspecting them and deeming them fit, she replaces them in the same order.

"Clean the mag too. Fill it up. Slap it in. When ready, pull back on the slide and it'll load."

"Where's the safety?"

"There's not a mechanical safety as such. It has a three-point safe action system that prevents accidental discharge. You'll feel it."

They fiddle with the vests. They're purposely bigger so they can each wear fleeces underneath them. They load them up, adding the penlights and extra batteries. Jo uses the drill and makes a hole through the end of the dowel, slips the rope through, ties it in a loop, melts the ends together and uses a strip of tape to hold it secure. The outcome is a Billy club with a wrist strap. Rough but effective.

It's almost one in the morning when everything is checked off, packed and ready to go. She tells Bertrand she needs to make a couple of phone calls. She'll join him soon. He climbs into bed, sets the alarm for three AM and is asleep when his head touches the pillows. It's been a long day.

With six hours difference, she knows Adam Thorne will be soon leaving for work at a little after seven in the morning back in Ottawa. He picks up on the second ring.

"Thorne here."

"Hello partner."

"Jo! Now, this is a surprise. Knowing you, I assume you're in trouble again?"

"Not at the moment but I'm planning on it.

"Can't stay clear, can you? Where are you?"

"I'm in Paris. And I need a favour."

"Of course you do. What is it?"

She explains the prostitution ring, how she got involved and what she's planning.

"I have their names and where they are from. Their handlers are threatening the families. Can you get a call out to the General Directorate for Countering Organized Crime? They have a human trafficking directorate. Tell them what's happening. I'll contact the Red Cross in Paris."

"How will I explain a Canadian cop calling the Romanian government for a sting operation in France?"

"I don't know, Adam. You're the one with the high IQ. Tell them it's a joint op."

"I'll have to bring in Maloney, he's still my boss."

"How's he feeling about me?"

"He thinks what you did was righteous but you're still wanted by people with more authority than him. It was his idea for me to go to Thailand and pick you up."

"Can you leave me out of it?"

"I doubt it. But he knows you are... or were a good cop, Jo. He does what his conscience tells him and it's usually always right."

"I'm leaving here in two and a half hours, and if all goes well I'll be dropping the women off at the Red Cross in the next seven to eight hours. I want to be sure there will be no repercussions in Romania."

"I can't guarantee anything, Jo."

"I know, Adam. I also know you will try your damn best."

There is a pause and neither want to say what is on their mind. He wants to tell her to walk away from this. To stay safe. But he knows she won't. She never backs down.

Jo misses her former partner. Aches for what once was.

"Goodbye, Adam. Thank you."

She hangs up before she gets all melancholy and starts blubbering. Composing herself, she dials the Red Cross office. Getting voice mail, she leaves a message that will certainly gain someone's attention soon enough. If not, she'll deal with it when she gets there with the women.

CHAPTER 16

At 3:45 AM Bertrand has all the lights off in his SUV when he pulls out of the tree line on Chemin Benôit. He's exposed on his right flank to the open fields. He needn't worry as there's nothing astir. A gibbous moon in a cloudless sky casts blue tones on the fields with long dark shadows to hide in. He backs the vehicle in the driveway of the abandoned farm as near to the house as he can so that the dark finish of his SUV blends with the night shadow of the house. The temperature has dropped to ten degrees Celsius. Jo and Bertrand leave their heavy jackets in the car. The thick fleeces and tactical vests are warm enough and do not confine their movement.

The yellowish light over the barn door of the second farm flickers as if it's dying; a warning maybe: Proceed with Caution. They move with stealth, creeping along the dark side of the road, which is cast in the shadows of the trees to their left. Dressed completely in black, no shiny surfaces to reflect light, they move unseen. The second house is far back from the road. Nothing moves, no cattle bellowing or dogs barking.

Coming over the rise, they can see lights from the house where the women are kept, one upstairs and one down. No yard lights. The homes are more than a century old, built with brick and fieldstone. The house is two storey with a one storey addition in the back. The long portion of the building is parallel to the driveway with the gable ends facing the woods and the road they came in on. The other faces a smaller outbuilding, a barn and the old silo.

Jo and Bertrand crouch behind a waist high hedgerow that separates the building from the road, inspecting the house and surroundings. The two windows upstairs are dark. A wide door is in the center of the lower level. A light is on in the room on the right. Jo wants to see in. A check of the yard shows there are two vehicles. One is the car the men were working on yesterday, and the other is similar but has been cannibalized for parts and sits on blocks with no wheels. The van is missing of course; in the city to pick up the young women.

An owl hoots from the forest behind them and startles them. Crouching down even more, Jo whispers to Bertrand.

"Hunting prey in the night. Like us."

He doesn't know if she's joking or serious. He says nothing. She swivels her mic into place and nods for him to do the same. Jo signals for him to wait.

"I'm going to peek in the window. Watch my back."

"Yeah I got it. Be careful, Jo."

The hedgerow has no leaves, just gangly limbs and broken fingers. It wouldn't hide her in the daylight but at night offers adequate cover. There is an opening in the bushes for a walkway. With little snow, she can feel the cobblestone under her feet when she hustles to the window on the right, crouches like a crab and drops in front of it. Peering up slowly, she has to look through a gauzy fabric and a dirty window. Everything she sees is blurry.

A table is in the middle of the floor and she can see movements of two people sitting at it. Their faces are obscure. The one facing her is bigger than the other. From the motion of their hands, she thinks they're playing cards. Relaxed. Good for her plan. She turns on her knees to face Bertrand. She can barely see him. Whispering into her mic she tells him what to do.

"I want you to circle around at the back of the house and come around the silo so you can pitch your smoke grenade at the car with no wheels. Do you see it?"

"*Oui*, yes."

"The noise will alert them, and the smoke confuse them. I can't be sure which door they'll come out. I expect this one or the one facing the driveway that doesn't look used much. I'm going back in the ditch. When they rush out to see what's happening, I'll toss the flashbang. Cover your ears and don't look at it. Then we run and subdue them. You got that?"

"Yes, going now."

She can see a shadow move along the hedge and disappear beyond the house. She sprints back to the ditch and plunks herself low, eyes trained on both exits. The smoke grenade should go in both. The distance from the silo to the car is about fifteen meters. Bertrand pulls the pin and steps into the open to throw the grenade. With no hood on the car, it lands in the open engine compartment. An audible pop gives way to a burst of white smoke. The men inside rush out the door facing the driveway with guns drawn. A slight breeze pushes the smoke toward the house and the men are soon enveloped in it. Jo stands and heaves the flashbang. It falls two meters from the men. She ducks back down and covers her ears.

At 170 decibels, the flashbang can cause hearing loss and tinnitus. Normal conversation averages sixty decibels. It flashes with an intensity of 7,000,000 candles. The men are stunned when it explodes. The men drop their weapons and hold their ears and eyes. One of them staggers and falls near the front door. Jo is already running. She speaks into her headset.

"You take the one by the door. I can't see the other one for the smoke but he must be close."

"Roger that."

Jo removes her baton from a loop on her belt and walks to the front of the building. No hurry. The men will be incapacitated. She can hear them groaning, and even though she doesn't understand the language, she's confident they're cursing. Bertrand reaches the smaller man by the door, who is scrabbling to stand up. He's sobbing from the pain and calling out to his partner. When Bertrand steps close, he knocks the man unconscious with a one-two punch. Jo finds the bigger man struggling on the ground. He's on his hands and knees, shaking his head. He doesn't hear Jo approach. She clips him on the back of the neck with the Billy club and he's down, doing them both a favour.

Ten minutes later, the men are bound, ankles and wrists, with duct tape. A wide strip across their mouths will keep them quiet. Jo makes sure they can still breathe. The door on the smaller outbuilding, some kind of tool shed, is open. Jo and Bertrand pull the unconscious bodies inside. They do a sweep through the house to be certain there is no one else around until they are satisfied they are alone. From a second storey window they can see a rim of light on the horizon from approaching headlights beyond the second farm. Jo waves to Bertrand.

"Go back behind the silo. You have your gun, the flashbangs. You're smart enough to know when to use them. I'll wait inside, take them by surprise. We need to watch for the women, don't put them in danger. We need to put the two men out."

She ducks inside and closes the door as the headlights come over the rise. What she doesn't know is there is a third man following the van.

CHAPTER 17

Jo enters the foyer; a closet is on the right with its door ajar. Opposite is an archway with a shower curtain strung halfway across, hiding the contents of the room. Beyond is a dark hallway. Kitchen on her left. A glance behind the curtain reveals an extra bedroom, which Jo thinks was once a living room. Two messy cots. A ceiling fan in the kitchen stirs smoke that drifted in the open door from the grenade. Jo stations herself at the top of the stairs where she can throw another flashbang if she has to. But not if the girls come in first.

She hates not having a better plan. Realizing the precarious position she's put, not only herself, but Bertrand into, she feels a moment of regret, of maybe this might her last gig. The image of the dead girl's graduation picture in the newspaper jars her back to her mission. It's too late now anyway.

The lights of the van glare through the windows as it pulls in front of the house. Jo gulps down her fear when a second set of headlights accompanies it. She didn't consider back up. Backing off might be a better option. She kneels to a shooting position and has the whole entryway in her line of sight. Nothing happens. Jo can't see the van but can hear the motor running, a squeaky fanbelt. The quiet unnerves her. She'll wait them out. It won't be long until they notice their buddies are not around or sleeping. The voice is deep, commanding, speaking French and Jo has no idea what he's saying. She senses a big man.

"Everyone be quiet. Nobody gets out. Something is amiss. Blow the horn."

The driver of the van bumps his fist producing sharp toots. A minute goes by. The same voice calls out, now angrier.

"Where's René and the Bear?"

He yells out their names. No response. Jo has snuck down the stairs and has slipped into the living room. She can peer out the edge of the window. The room is dark and so is she. A boxy, tough looking truck, like a Jeep, sits beside the van. To the right of the four-wheel drive, shielded by the open door is a tall man, bushy beard, wide of shoulders. Jo can't make out any other facial features but he has long hair. Something glints off his face when he moves. She listens but other voices are muffled, only his standing out.

"Ronaldo, go in and see. Clément, check the back. You woman, shut up!"

He draws a gun from inside his jacket, waves it at the girls first who go totally mute. He braces himself behind the truck fender and points his weapon at the front door. Jo sees a hooded man, face hidden, approach the house, with his gun drawn. Stocky and shorter than average, he's uncertain and nervous. She can see the gun wavering. Each step is tentative as if he's walking through mines. Jo hurries over behind the opaque curtain and makes a slit for one eye on the far edge. The door slowly opens.

Bertrand is watching the other man come closer as he circles the buildings, goes around the house, returns, and then circles the barn. He is about to come around the silo when something clatters in the tool shed behind him. Bertrand panics and throws a flashbang. He drops down with hands clasped tight over his ears and eyes scrunched shut. It lands right at the man's feet. He goes blind and deaf in milliseconds. The blinding light gets a few of the girls, the noise gets everyone. It is not so bad in the van but it still hurts.

The big man crouches down by the fender, saved from the fierce glare and bang by the van. Jo recoils and falls to the floor, on her knees. The stone walls muffle the noise and protect her from the light although her ears are ringing. The man at the door got a full blast of the noise. The gun flies out of his hands, which automatically go to his ears. The women are all screaming and holding each other.

With the groaning man two meters away, Jo flies out the front door. Using all the swing she can muster, she clubs him in the stomach. Most of his innards shut down momentarily and in his stunned state, she

86

whacks him on the temple, without even disturbing the hood and he flops over like a dead cobra. Before she can move, a bullet hits her directly in the chest. The force of the impact knocks her flat on her back a whole two meters away.

Thinking her dead, *Le Tigre* walks slowly toward her with his gun pointing at her. When he's almost standing over her and raising his gun to fire, a shot rings out from the silo. The 9mm bullet obliterates his left foot. The next one hits the dirt a few centimeters away from his other foot. He pivots on the good one, ignoring the pain and hops to the Land Rover. Throwing it in gear, using his good foot, he reverses, spinning and slewing until he gets it turned and rushes down the road. No one can hear him cursing and yelling from the pain.

Bertrand races to Jo's side with Tanya right behind him and the other women close by. Kneeling by her, Bertrand picks the slug off the vest. He brushes the curls from Jo's forehead; the toque and headset having flown off. He takes his own hat off and makes a pillow to keep her off the cold ground. She begins to groan and roll her head back and forth. One hand is clutched to her chest while she props herself up on one elbow.

"Oh, it hurts."

Bertrand smiles widely with relief.

"Better to hurt than to be dead. You are a crazy woman."

She pulls on him until she's sitting. He helps her stand up.

"Where did the jeep go?"

"I shot at the bugger. He was yelling and by the way he was hopping, I think I hit him in the foot. Guess he thought it best to leave."

"In the foot?"

"I was aiming for his body, but..., you know, I was kind of nervous."

Jo giggles at his antics as she shakes her head.

"Good move on the flashbang. My ears are still humming. Thank goodness I was inside.

He shrugs and holds out his hands to give her a hug. She owes him.

"Thank you, my brave friend. Now let's get the girls a new home."

Tanya is next to hug her and comments on her fears.

"What of our families? My brother and parents?"

Jo puts a hand on her shoulder and stares at her directly.

"I'll explain it all to you soon. Tell the girls to pack what they need, not too much, just one bag. And tell them to hurry. Whoever that man was, he'll be alerting someone."

Tanya looks at Jo with wide eyes, a look of astonishment.

"That was *Le Tigre*, the Tiger. He's a terrible, evil man. He tells everyone what to do. He will be looking for us."

"He won't be able to find you. Trust me."

Jo watches Tanya explain what is happening. Several women are whooping and waving their hands at their freedom. The others exclaim their fears. Tanya points to Jo and reassures them it will work out. The women rush to the house. In less than ten minutes all of them are filing into the van, hoping it's the last time in that place. They've changed into jeans or trousers, sweaters and jackets, with an eclectic group of carryalls. Short skirts, glossy tops, feathery boas, skimpy jackets, and gaudy jewellery remain left behind in their bedrooms. No IDs.

Jo gets the girls quieted down and directs Bertrand behind the wheel of the van. She's sitting in the front passenger seat and when the van comes over the first rise, she points down the road.

"Drop me off at your SUV and I'll follow you. The address is 21 rue de la Vanne. You know where that is?"

"Roughly, but I'll find it."

Jo turns back to Tanya, who is in the seat behind her. She has question marks all over her face. All the women do. They stare at her. Anticipation. Fear. Bewilderment. Joy. They are all beautiful.

"We're taking you to the Red Cross. They will arrange places for you to stay and will be working to get you back home. People will be reaching out to your families. We'll be there soon."

Tanya translates for those who need it. There's a communal sigh. Clapping and laughter. Except one, and the women go quiet when she speaks out in English.

"What about the police?"

Jo has to think for a minute before she replies. The police will be involved soon enough. She saw more lights on in the second house. They'll have heard the grenades. The women may be back in Romania before the police figure things out.

"I can't tell you what will happen. No one knows where you will be. It's up to you."

Bertrand turns in to the first driveway, the headlights exposing his BMW. He removes the keys from his pocket.

"Here, stay close when we enter the city fringe. I don't want to lose you."

She sees in his eyes that his words are not about a car ride. She reaches over and squeezes his hand just as the sun rises out of a hazy mist. It could be a romantic moment if not for their urgent situation. Jumping out, she runs for the SUV. Bertrand turns the van around, Jo following close behind. She can't stop smiling all the way to Paris.

CHAPTER 18

The Red Cross found homes for the rescued women amongst staff and volunteers. They receive a large donation from an anonymous source, pegged for the care of the women and covering their airfare home. Tanya and two other women do speak to the police about their unbearable forced existence of lust and greed and fear. The next day, two other groups of enslaved women are freed, sixteen in all. Twelve members of the Killing Cross are in jail awaiting arraignment. Two more are dead.

Adam Thorne did indeed speak to a counterpart in Romania, with Maloney's approval. He didn't ask where the lead came from. He knew. He trusted the source. Boris Albescu is with the Directorate of Human Trafficking in Romania. They hold similar ranks within their respective organizations but Albescu has responsibility for a much larger territory and more headaches. The schemes luring young women to foreign countries, and the people behind them, is at the top of his list. He has assured Maloney the families will be watched.

Oswald Bouthillier, better known as Le Tigre, is sitting in the den of the Lagrange mansion. It's big enough to hold two dozen full size autos. There is enough seating for twenty people with various couches and chairs arranged around a blazing fireplace and pool table. Bookshelves and bragging memorabilia line the walls. A bar dominates one corner, a command post another. A wide desk with ornate legs and polished wood takes up a great part of the section. Behind it sits an old man. Not a slouched shoulders old man, but a vibrant powerful old man. Antonin Lagrange's shoulders are proud and square. He has thick silver hair pushed back to the collar of his dark suit and a thin beard is as white as paper, amplifying the steel grey in his eyes. The snarl is meant only for Le Tigre.

Bouthillier sits in a plush velvet chair directly in front of the desk. To the right, behind the desk is the man in the suit, Brandy's tormentor, the presumed heir, a younger version of the owner without the same grit in his jaw. Instead he projects an attitude of being overconfident and spoiled. To the left is one of the biggest men Bouthillier has ever been around. Over two meters, he is one hundred and forty kilos of muscle, displaying a shaved dome covered in scars. His eyes are far apart and his nose has a history of violence. Rumours of his wrath and methods of torture cause Bouthillier to shiver when the man's stare bores into him. He's starting to feel nervous. He didn't think The Crusher would be here. The old man waves to the younger Lagrange and points at a carafe of liquor at the edge of a sideboard beside a tray with crystal whisky glasses.

Pouring two fingers into three glasses, he gives one to senior Lagrange, one to Bouthillier and returns behind his father, sipping his. The old man offers Bouthillier a toast.

"Salut!"

Bouthillier offers up his glass. His shaking hand makes wavelets in the liquor. He drains the liquor. Antonin is happy to see the man nervous. It suits his purpose. He leans back in his leather chair and steeples his fingers, his elbows on the arms.

"You've cost us a deep cut in our revenues, Oswald. Twenty-five prostitutes who are not working for us, or you, anymore. It won't affect me too much overall. I've adequate means to lay low until the dust settles. But you, Oswald, how will you afford your rich tastes, your little troop of psychopaths and misfits you call bikers, most of them now in jail. Your estate in the country, your fancy motorcycles. Huh?"

"It's not my… "

"Shut up! I'm not finished. You will speak only when I ask you a question."

Le Tigre acts more like Le Chat and crouches into his chair.

"All you had to do was look after the sluts. Keep them in line. Threaten them a little. Collect the money. Protect our investment. Now we are out over twenty-four thousand euros… your 20% is gone."

Antonin lets his temper settle. The younger Lagrange stares at

Bouthillier with a smirk. Le Chat stays quiet and the giant continues to glare at him.

"I'm replacing you as head of the gang. But don't fear, Oswald, I have another position for you, something more suited to your aggressive attitude. I think you'll be happy. Won't he, Albert?"

The son only nods. He knows what his father is offering the man. Bouthillier is fooled by their phony smiles. He relaxes, knowing how loyal he's been to the family. It has to count for something. He stands with his empty glass, pointing at the carafe. The older man rolls his chair back. Out of the way. The sideboard to his left. Albert steps back as well.

"Yes, drink up Oswald."

Bouthillier walks around the front of the desk and to the carafe. With his back to the trio, he pours himself a drink. The glass only has an inch left in it when the carafe falls from his grasp. Vice-like fingers are wrapped around his throat and start to squeeze. It only takes a fraction of a second for him to realize what is happening. He starts to pull at the hand and feels himself slowly lifted from the floor. His kicks uselessly at the timbers behind him, claws the skin off the hands which are taking his life. Unable to breath, his arms go limp. The last image he sees before his eyes go out of focus is a photo hanging on the wall of Antonin and some dignitary shaking hands. The deal has been sealed.

After a moment of stillness, when he is certain of death, the Crusher drops the dead body on the floor in front of the desk. The old man rises from his chair to peer down at his soldier's bleeding hand. Looking up at the giant with a twisted fondness, he removes the handkerchief from his breast pocket and holds it to the scratches.

"See Mariline in the kitchen, mon ami. She will look after your hand."

Then to his son.

"Get rid of the garbage."

CHAPTER 19

After getting the women to the Red Cross, Bertrand dumped the hardware, packed a suitcase and left four postdated cheques to cover the rent for his landlady, saying he would be out of the city for an indefinite amount of time, probably until late spring. He contacted one of his friends and left a key, asking him to check on the premises occasionally and water his collection of cacti. Jo gathered her belongings and said a fond goodbye to Max and Aurora. On their way out of the city, they dropped Brandy at the airport. She was giving up on her dream and heading for South Africa.

Jo and Bertrand are cruising on the A6 southbound. With a pit stop in Crèancey, they expect to get to Lyon by early evening. The farther they get from Paris, the more relaxed and happier they become. The decision to escape the uncertainty and risk of staying in the city was easy. They talk about everything. They analyze their escapade; what they might've done differently, what they did well. The retelling of Le Tigre getting shot in his foot and him dancing back to his truck provokes hearty laughter, so much that Bertrand has to pull over on the shoulder of the road until he stops laughing.

They take the Crèancey exit off the A6 and bypass McDonalds to have lunch at a pub-like local eatery. Bertrand introduces her to Cassoulet, a bean and meat dish. Like a thick soup of bacon, sausage and chicken in the rich mixture of cubes of carrot, slices of celery, diced tomatoes and tangy onions. Delicious. They each have a glass of Kronenbourg 1664. Bertrand explains to her it's named after the year it was first brewed. The brew masters continue to use the same recipe.

93

A third one is split between them. They also share a piece of apple pie with ice cream and fresh coffees.

Jo teases him with her fork, pushing it away from the pie. She forgets any regrets, any attachment to her past. She feels weightless with Bertrand. A comfort unknown for a long time. She feels lightheaded when he smiles at her.

"We should hit the road, *ma chèrie*, if we want to get to Lyon at a decent hour."

Jo gives him *a thumbs up* and finishes her coffee. She offers to drive for a while if she only has to stay on the highway. He agrees and gets her on the proper ramp and in the right direction. Adjusting the seat, he reclines in a more comfortable position.

"Wake me in one hour. Or if you get sleepy. We've been up since three this morning"

Jo assures him she's fine but that she'll be glad for a bed, a romantic dinner, she hopes, and lots of cuddles. Bertrand takes the wheel at a rest area. They get to Lyon, or rather the outskirts of Lyon, shortly after eight in the evening. In Caluire-et-Cuire they register at an auberge which has a small restaurant attached. Freshening up first, they dine slowly on roast duck and vegetables, a bottle of *Chateauneuf-du-pape* and peach cobbler. With the last of their energy and the glow of the booze, they begin to strip as soon as they're at the doorway and continue all the way to the bed, littering the floor with their clothing. Their passion is heightened by unfamiliarity as they explore sensitive areas with fingertips and kisses. They prolong release, basking in new sensations, unwilling for it to end. Finally, spent from blissful release and an exhaustive day, they spoon into each other and are soon asleep.

The next day, the journey through the Alps often stops the conversation as they make the sharp turns on the valley floor to be treated to majestic view after majestic view. Jo opens up about her father and sheds a few tears when she talks about leaving Canada. He's stunned into silence. He knows she's tough but can't imagine what she must've gone through. He talks about the loss of his wife and son, never having opened his heart up to anyone before. The conversation and drive are therapeutic for both of them. The ensuing silence brings comfort. They arrive before the sun goes down.

Bertrand's house in Villeneuve-Loubet is a charming, stuccoed cottage-like building, storey and a half with fancy dormers on the front roof. Baby blue shutters frame the windows. A weathervane sticks up from the edge of the chimney. The rooster tipped sideways stops it from making a complete circle; it can only pivot back and forth, no matter what the direction of the wind. It is kind of like how Jo feels at present when she sees it, not knowing which direction her life should take.

By the time they've unpacked their suitcases, *Le Tigre* has been dead for several hours. Jo will never find out, nor will she care. Tired from the long drive, they dine on some of the best fish and chips Jo has ever eaten. Afterwards, they take hot showers and make it an early night. The next morning, their coffee is long forgotten as they caress each other's bodies, discovering ticklish places. Their lovemaking is playful and romantic amid the early morning sunshine that fills the bedroom.

Of the next four days Jo can only explain her feelings as if they have come from heaven. The mornings find them curled up in tight embraces. They laze about in housecoats, Jo's too big, while Bertrand tends to his bets, his clients, the odds and payouts. She meets his aunt when they have lunch with her. They visit Nice to see the museums and walk the beach in bundled jackets. He takes her on a day trip to Monaco where Jo learns to play blackjack and with a beginner's luck, leaves three hundred euros richer. Bertrand on the other hand, loses fifty. Dining in tiny cafes, watching the sunset over the Mediterranean, dancing until their feet hurt in a posh cabaret, the day goes by too quickly before they drive back at two in the morning, the backseat full of souvenirs and heads full of memories.

One day it rains. Jo and Bertrand have their breakfast in bed in the nude. They play cribbage, the winner getting an orgasm so nobody loses. Jo leaves Bertrand to his business and discovers a book by American author, MJ LaBeff. Jo loves thrillers and detective stories; the blurb shows promise. She stretches out on the couch and is enthralled from the beginning. As intriguing as it is, Jo gives in to the excitement of the last few days and dozes off.

Waking an hour later, she does so with a start. A bad dream shocks her. Sitting up and rubbing her eyes, the book falls to the floor. She looks around as if she doesn't remember where she is, her surroundings unfamiliar. Bertrand's voice from an upstairs office brings her back to reality. She holds her head in her hands, her eyes out of focus. In her dream they were dancing, laughing, so happy and suddenly a bunch of bikers tear through the crowd and shoot Bertrand. He fell away from her in slow motion and his eyes cried out. The barrel of a pistol in her face woke her up. It chills her and she shudders. It's a message or an omen she thinks. His life could be in danger.

Jo can't stop thinking of him taking the bullet. She's disturbed by Bertrand rushing from upstairs, fully dressed. But when she looks up at him something lights up his eyes and she puts on a convincing smile. He throws her a kiss and goes to the closet by the front door to get his coat.

"I have to go for a couple of hours, *chèrie*. I made an appointment at the dealer where I bought my auto and it needs servicing. I'll pick up something for later. Is calamari okay?"

She dreads what she's thinking, but for his sake she throws it off and with a heart full of happiness and sadness, she hugs him tightly. He's surprised for a second but returns the gesture. They sway for a few seconds until she kisses him softly, feeling his moustache upon her skin, the tenderness of his lips. Stepping back, she thinks of all his good qualities and can't help beaming.

"Calamari sounds fine."

"*Bon.* I'll see you soon."

As soon as he leaves, she goes to the laundry area in the downstairs bathroom where her clothes have stopped in the dryer. She hangs the robe she borrowed from Bertrand on a hook on the door. She dons her jeans and loose sweater over her favourite Wonder Woman T-shirt. Going to the bedroom they shared, she retrieves her suitcase, as well as the few toiletries she left in his bathroom. Back in the laundry area, she folds and packs her clothes, fitting everything in one carryall and one backpack. Both bulge from the things she bought in France. When she has everything ready, she looks for something to write on. She can't leave without saying goodbye. In his office is a letter size scratch pad and pencils, lots of pencils. She takes it downstairs where she can sit at the table.

My dearest Bertrand,

Thank you from the bottom of my heart for the most fabulous days of my life. I don't think I deserve such happiness. I hate to say goodbye this way, Bertrand, but I would not be able to tell you in person. I have to be careful. I could fall in love with a guy like you. You're magnificent… in every way.

But I fear for your future with me around. Stay put in this little paradise you have here. Wait it out and you will be able to return to Paris again. I have my own ghosts to purge. Don't try to follow me. At the time of writing, I'm still

not sure where I'm going. I'll write. I have your address.
   I adore you. xo
   J.

She tears off the sheet, folds it in half and places it on the floor in the entryway where he'll be sure to see it. After getting her boots on, she puts on her jacket and toque, tightens the straps on her backpack, grabs her suitcase, and leaves. She walks all the way to the coast where businesses and cafes line the street. It's not long before she's able to hail a cab. In her broken French, she asks to be taken to the airport.

The driver is a small man with stray hairs across a bald dome and dark glasses. His smile almost appears too big for his face. It's a damn fine fare. *L'Aéroport Nice Côte d'Azur* is twenty minutes west of Nice. He might even be able to snag something on the way back.

He talks her head off the whole time even though she doesn't understand him. He asks her questions but when she doesn't answer he gives a small laugh and carries on. She realizes he likes the sound of his own voice and ignores him, trying to decide where she's going. Uncertainty follows her and by the time they arrive, she decides to roll the dice. The first vacation or destination poster she sees, that is where she will go. Feeling good, she tips the driver too much and he's agog at her generosity.

Waving goodbye, she tightens her collar. The wind is stronger here and it's chilly. She follows a small crowd getting off a shuttle bus and when she enters the departure area, posters are plastered on the walls and pedestals. The one that catches her eye is of a giant tawny face with traditional tattoos and a warrior's forceful stare. Under the poster is the word, MAORI, in large, stylized letters. Jo walks closer to study the image. The pitch invites travellers to visit New Zealand.

ABOUT THE AUTHOR

Allan Hudson lives in Dieppe, New Brunswick, Canada, with his wife Gloria. This is his tenth publication since starting to write in his early 50s.

Happily retired, he spends most mornings writing and publishing his blog – South Branch Scribbler. The rest of his days are spent with important issues, such as napping and goofing off.

You can contact him as follows:

Email – sbscribbler@gmail.com

410-3400 Principale Ouest, Dieppe, NB E1A 9E7

www.southbranchscribbler.ca

Allan Hudson Author | Facebook

twitter.com/hudson_allan

www.goodreads.com/allanhudson

Manufactured by Amazon.ca
Bolton, ON